DANGER IN PARIS

Fearing their marriage is dying, Beth follows vague, inattentive Dan on his business trip to Paris, hoping to surprise him. But the surprise is on her when she discovers that Dan has been living a secret life that she never once suspected. As she finds herself plunged into a terrifying world of guns and cat-and-mouse pursuits, Beth's only companion is a husband who, following a car crash, can no longer remember anything about her, their children, what he does for a living, or even who they can trust . . .

Books by Ken Preston
in the Linford Romance Library:

FATE IN FREEFALL

KEN PRESTON

DANGER IN PARIS

Complete and Unabridged

LINFORD
Leicester

First published in Great Britain in 2015

First Linford Edition
published 2016

A catalogue record for this book is available
from the British Library.

ISBN 978–1–4448–2768–2

Published by
F. A. Thorpe (Publishing)
Anstey, Leicestershire

Set by Words & Graphics Ltd.
Anstey, Leicestershire
Printed and bound in Great Britain by
T. J. International Ltd., Padstow, Cornwall

This book is printed on acid-free paper

1

Beth Ogilvy did not like the way her husband was looking at her.

Granted, she had just given him a big surprise, and no doubt it was taking a few moments to sink in. But still, the way he was looking at her, she didn't like it.

Not one bit.

Usually he didn't give her any kind of 'look' at all. He was always so distracted, thinking about work, or catching up with the news, or writing his reports on that laptop he carried everywhere. No, whatever anyone might say about Dan Ogilvy, it wouldn't be that he gave people a 'look'.

Especially Beth.

In fact, some days it seemed to Beth that he didn't even notice her presence.

That hadn't been the case when they were first married. Dan used to look at his wife all the time back then, and all her friends and family often remarked on how he was so in love. It was obvious, they said, that he doted on his new wife, just by the way he constantly gazed at her.

Beth enjoyed all the attention he lavished on her, and her friends were right, he was utterly and helplessly in love. Every day she saw that devotion in his eyes, in his expression, and she loved him back, just as intensely.

But then, as happens in all marriages, the years passed by, children arrived (two in their case: a girl first, and then a boy two years later), and the mortgage grew bigger, along with their responsibilities and a sense that life was passing them by. The children grew up and went through junior school, and then secondary school, and became increasingly independent.

Beth gave up full-time work (as a teacher) to become a full-time mum, and then went back to work part-time. Dan left his job at the university, where he had been teaching social studies, and got himself a new position working for an obscure government department, which mainly seemed to involve writing papers and presenting them at conferences around the world. Beth had never quite been able to explain to herself, let alone anybody else who asked, what her husband actually did, but it certainly kept him busy.

And as the years passed, the looks he gave her faded in intensity, and became less frequent. Until finally Beth realised one day that they had gone a whole week without exchanging a single word, or looking at each other once.

Well, that's to be expected, she had thought as she stood in the kitchen, holding in her arms a pile of damp clothes she had just pulled from the washing machine. *We're a busy family, and we both work, and Dan's job takes him away all the time. And isn't this what happens to all marriages in the end? After all, neither of you are giggly teenagers anymore.*

Beth stepped outside, the autumnal sunshine warm on her face, and began hanging the washing on the line. A grey mass of despair had filled her chest. Had their marriage died without them realising it? Had they been so busy bringing up a family, they simply hadn't noticed the love between them fading, and finally disappearing?

Was it possible that they were no longer in love?

No, she thought. *It's true that we're not a pair of giggly teenagers anymore, but that's a good thing. The love we have for each other is stronger than that, and has bound us together through some challenging times. We simply don't express it the way we used to, but that has to change, before we drift apart completely.*

That day, standing in the garden, hanging out the washing, Beth decided she needed to put some interest and excitement back into their marriage.

★   ★   ★

Over the next few weeks she tried talking to Dan, tried paying him more attention. But the only responses she got from him were some grunts from behind his newspaper and a couple of curious glances.

Beth decided she needed to work harder at revitalising their marriage.

She booked a romantic weekend away in Scotland, but Dan had to cancel at the last minute due to work. She bought herself some sexy new nightwear, but he was too tired and distracted to notice. She made him a wonderful meal for their anniversary, and bought expensive chocolates and champagne, but he phoned home and said he had to stay late at the office.

Finally, as the nights drew in and Christmas approached, Beth gave in and admitted defeat. Their marriage had obviously been suffering a long, slow, lingering death over the years. Despite her recent attempts to save it, she finally had to admit that their marriage was dead, and not even a miracle could bring it back to life.

'Oh, Beth, no!' Sara had said when she'd told her. 'I know Dan can be a boring old fuddy-duddy sometimes; and yes, he's totally obsessed with work. But he still loves you, I know he does.'

Beth's sister, at twenty-seven, was eleven years younger than Beth. Sara always liked to joke that she was the mistake, but in truth their parents had been trying for a brother or sister for Beth for many years, and had given up just as her mother became pregnant with Sara.

The two sisters were sitting in the conservatory of Beth and Dan's semi-detached home, in a quiet backwater street in Aylesbury. Jess, the elderly cat, was curled up on a cushion, sharing the wicker settee with Beth. The family got him from a rescue home a few months after Sophie, their eldest, was born and he was named after Postman Pat's cat. Now fourteen, he spent his days sleeping and eating, and then sleeping some more. Beth often envied him the simplicity of his life.

Sara sat opposite, looking cool in her trendily baggy top and artfully ripped jeans, her hair tied up, and wearing large, heavy-rimmed glasses. Beth felt much less trendy in her old faded jeans and comfortable warm sweater. Her dark, curly hair was tied back, and Beth was acutely aware of how tired and drained she must look. They both held mugs of steaming tea in their cupped hands.

Beth still thought of her little sister as exactly that: a little girl running around and being alternately adorable and annoying.

Where had all the years disappeared to?

Even her own two children had grown up, with Toby, their youngest, about to take that step into his teenage years on his next birthday.

Beth felt as though her life was slipping away in a drudgery of washing and cleaning.

'I don't know if he does still love me,' Beth said, dabbing at her eyes. 'I'm just a part of the furniture now, as far as Dan's concerned. If I left today, it would probably take him a week to notice I was gone, and then only because the fridge would be empty.'

She hadn't meant to cry, but speaking her thoughts out loud suddenly made it all seem so much more real.

'Oh Beth, don't cry,' Sara said. 'Is it really that bad?'

'I'm sorry,' Beth said. 'I can't help it. It only seems ten minutes ago we were desperately in love, and we had Sophie, and then Toby, and we were a family, and we were so happy.' Beth paused, took a sip of her tea. 'And then they both grew up.'

'But that's a good thing, right?' Sara said. 'Now that you've got some independence back, you and Dan can go getting all romantic again. Why don't you book a nice, cosy romantic weekend somewhere?'

Beth sighed. 'I've already tried that,

but Dan cancelled it, and spent the weekend in the office.'

'Beth, this isn't like you at all. You've got to get tough with him, show him who's boss.' Sara took a sip of her tea. 'You can't drift apart any more. It would be hideous if you two got divorced.'

'Who's getting divorced?'

Toby was standing in the doorway to the conservatory, in full football kit including boots, and holding a dirty football in his hands.

'Toby!' Beth exclaimed. 'How many times have I told you not to wear your football boots in the house?'

'Who's getting divorced?' Toby said again.

'No one. Where are you off to?'

Toby rolled his eyes. 'Where do you think, Mum? I'm meeting Will and Oliver down the park for a game of football.'

'Mum!' Sophie stormed into the conservatory, shoving Toby out of the way.

9

'Watch it!' Toby snapped.

'Toby's been on my Facebook account, and he's pretended to be me and said I fancy Ben Appleton!' Sophie yelled, pointing at Toby, her finger almost jabbing him in the face.

'Well, you do,' Toby said, grinning. 'I was doing you a favour. You'll never ask him out otherwise.'

Beth sighed. 'All right, you two, I'll sort this out later. Me and your Auntie Sara are having a talk right now.'

'Mum and Dad are getting divorced,' Toby said.

'No! You can't!' Sophie shouted, her eyes wide.

'Don't be silly, no one's talking about divorce,' Beth said, and thought, *not yet, anyway*.

'Yeah, right,' Toby said. 'Then why did I hear — '

'Out!' Beth shouted, pointing to the door. 'We'll talk about this later.'

'Bye, guys,' Sara said, giving them a wave and a smile.

'Bye, Auntie Sara,' the two children

said, and left the conservatory, still bickering.

'They're adorable,' Sara said.

'They're a pain in the backside,' Beth replied.

Sara sighed. 'Why don't you talk to Dan tonight, before he goes away on this business trip? Tell him how unhappy you are, that things need to change. You can't carry on like this.'

'No, it's too late; he wouldn't listen. He hasn't listened to me in years.'

'Oh, Beth!' Sara snapped. 'You sound like you've given up on him and your marriage already. Pull yourself together, and stop moping about. I'm not going to let you split up with Dan; that would just be awful. You'd most likely have to sell the house, and he would end up living in a bedsit, and then who would look after him? I mean, don't get me wrong; you know how much I love Dan — he's adorable — but he's not exactly the most practical man on the planet, is he? If he was living on his own he'd probably forget to feed himself, or wash, or clean his teeth. You know what he's like — always got his head buried in a book or some big fat report from the institute of boring clever people.'

Beth put her mug of tea on the glass-topped table, slumped back in the chair, and let out a helpless groan. 'But this is what I'm talking about!' she said. 'He's become so boring and dull and immersed in his work, he's not the man I married anymore. He used to be so much fun, so lively and full of surprises.'

'You should book a romantic break somewhere for Christmas,' Sara said. 'After all, it's your wedding anniversary on Christmas Eve. Wouldn't it be lovely, just the two of you? I can see you both now, cuddled up together in front of a log fire somewhere remote and beautiful, while it snows outside.'

'Can't,' Beth said glumly. 'Dan's already going away for work tomorrow. He's not even sure he'll be back home in time for Christmas Day.'

'Oooohhh!' Sara shouted in frustration. 'He can't work over Christmas. I mean, it's not right! It's . . . it's . . . '

'Christmas, I know,' Beth sighed.

'And it's your wedding anniversary! That man is hopeless! Where's he going — has he told you?'

'Paris, of all places.' Beth looked out at her garden. It looked so beautiful in the summer months, so lush and colourful. But now the trees were bare, and the flowers had died, and everything looked so cold and depressed beneath the grey sky. 'We used to talk about going to Paris together, one day. He said he would take me to the top of the Eiffel Tower on our wedding anniversary one day, and he would kiss me, overlooking the most romantic city in the world.'

'Go with him,' Sara said firmly.

'I can't,' Beth replied, ruffling Jess's ears.

'Why not?'

'I already suggested it to him, and he told me he would love to have me and the children there, but he was going to be too busy. Something about a

13

presentation he has to do, and some research into something or other.'

Jess lifted his head off the seat and looked at Beth. He started purring.

'But surely even Dan wouldn't be working on Christmas Day! Tell you what — why don't you go, but not tell him. And don't take the children; that would hardly be the romantic break you need, now, would it?'

Beth stopped tickling Jess behind his ears and looked at her sister. Jess lay his head back down on the cushion and closed his eyes.

'I can't do that. Who would look after Tobes and Sophie?'

'I can. I'll come and stay, and we'll have a fantastic time, and we'll most likely be going to Mum and Dad's for Christmas Day anyway.'

Beth shook her head. 'No, I can't.'

'Yes you can. Find out where he's staying, and you could surprise him at the hotel. That way he would have to spend some time with you.'

'No, that's ridiculous,' Beth said,

shaking her head again.

'Oh, Beth, what's the worst that could happen?' Sara said, a hint of exasperation in her voice.

'Well, he might, um . . . I suppose he could . . . Oh I don't know. He'd probably just send me straight back home again.'

'Listen to yourself. You go on about how boring Dan is, and how the excitement has left your marriage; but you're the one sitting here in dull, boring Aylesbury, moaning, while your husband will be spending Christmas in Paris!'

'You make it sound like he'll be having fun,' Beth said.

'Maybe he will.'

A tiny worm of suspicion and unease wriggled its way into Beth's mind. 'You make it sound like . . . like he might be having an affair,' she whispered.

'Oh, of course he's not having an affair,' Sara said. She leaned forward in her seat and reached across the table and took Beth's hands. 'Why don't I

15

make you another cup of tea, and we can go on the laptop and look at flights to Paris. Come on, it will be an adventure.'

'Well, I suppose . . . ' Beth said, and smiled at her sister. 'Maybe we could visit the Eiffel Tower after all, and have that romantic kiss on Christmas Eve. Being our anniversary, it would be a little like renewing our vows.' Beth looked wistfully out at the garden again, thinking about how dull and lifeless it was, but how in the spring it would begin to bloom once more. 'It could be a new start for us.'

'Well there you go, that's settled then. But we've got to keep this a secret from Dan, right? The thing is to surprise him with it when you're out there. And I bet he'll be so pleased to see you, you'll have a fantastic time, and this will be just the tonic you both need. I just wish I could be there to see the look on his face when he sees you.'

★ ★ ★

Standing in the foyer of the Prince de Galles hotel, her suitcase on the floor beside her, Beth was glad Sara wasn't here to see the look on Dan's face. The initial puzzlement and surprise had quickly given way to what looked like anger.

'Beth, what on earth are you doing here?' he said.

He was wearing an expensive-looking suit, one she wasn't aware of ever seeing in his wardrobe, and he held himself in a certain way she had never noticed before. His dark brown hair was swept back, and he was tall and broad shouldered, and looking more handsome than Beth had remembered for a long time. Perhaps it was the luxurious surroundings of the hotel (and really, wasn't this a bit grand for a business trip?), but Dan looked different somehow.

'Surprise!' Beth said, in a rather weak and pathetic voice. She tried smiling, but the smile disappeared as Dan's face darkened even more with anger.

'Beth, I don't understand,' he said. 'Please tell me what you're doing here, right now.'

A bellboy hurried up and picked up Beth's suitcase.

'*Voulez-vous que de prendre votre valise pour votre chambre, madame?*' he said.

'Oh, I'm sorry, I don't speak French,' Beth replied, suddenly flustered.

'He wants to know if he can take your suitcase to your room,' Dan said. 'I think not.'

He turned to the bellboy and said something to him in French, reaching into his jacket and pulling out a wallet. He passed the boy some euros. The bellboy took the money and put the suitcase down and walked away, smiling.

Beth looked at Dan in astonishment. 'I didn't know you could speak French!'

'Beth, I have no idea what's got into you, but we need to book you a flight back to England right now. What were you thinking of, flying out here to surprise me like this?'

Dan picked up her suitcase and took her by the arm, leading her to the imposing reception desk, staffed by equally imposing men and women, looking like they had stepped out of a Hollywood film from the 1940s.

Dan spoke in rapid, fluent French to a lady on the desk. She picked up a phone and spoke into it.

'What's she doing?' Beth said.

'Booking you a seat on the next flight home,' Dan replied, grimly.

He was still holding onto her arm, and Beth, suddenly angry, twisted free of him.

She leaned over the marble topped desk, snatched the telephone from the startled concierge, and slammed it back in place.

'Now you look here,' she snapped, turning to face her husband. 'I've come all the way out here to surprise you with a romantic Christmas break, and what do you do? You try and send me right back home on the next available flight!'

Dan's expression softened slightly as he saw how upset his wife was. 'Beth, I — '

'Don't!' Beth shouted, holding up a hand. 'I don't want to hear it! These last few years you've obviously preferred spending your time at work rather than with me, and now I can see why. I didn't know the government splashed out on luxury hotels abroad for lowly civil servants.'

'Lowly civil — ?'

'Looks like you've been leading the high life while I've been sat at home, worrying about how hard they make you work, and how dull it must be, and how you must miss your family so much. If only I'd known the truth!'

Beth, her face flushed with anger, realised she was in danger of bursting into tears. The last thing she wanted was for Dan to see her crying. She spun around, ready to stalk away, forgetting about her suitcase and not thinking about where she might go.

But she didn't manage even one step, as there was a tall, beautiful woman standing right behind her.

'Oh!' Beth gasped, in surprise.

The woman was slender, with a smooth, lightly tanned complexion, high cheekbones, and long, luxurious dark hair. She wouldn't have looked out of place on a catwalk.

'Daniel?' she said, glancing over Beth's shoulder. 'Is everything all right?'

'Tamara, um, this is Beth,' Dan said. 'My wife.'

'Oh, I see,' Tamara replied, her voice cool and distant.

Beth spun back round to face her husband, the tears finally spilling over her lids and down her cheeks.

'You're having an affair!'

2

'Don't be silly, Beth, of course I'm not having an affair!' Dan snapped.

Beth took an involuntary step back, shocked at Dan's sharp tone. In all their years of marriage, he'd never spoken to her like this. Unfortunately, in stepping back, she trod on Tamara's foot.

'Ouch!' Tamara screeched. 'Watch what you're doing, you absurd little woman!'

Before Beth had chance to move, or even think of a suitably barbed response to being called an 'absurd little woman', Tamara had shoved her to one side. Beth staggered, and tripped, and headed for the floor. Fortunately her suitcase broke her fall, and she simply sat down rather abruptly on top of it.

'Daniel, this is not the time or place for a marital tiff,' Tamara said, looking at Dan and ignoring Beth as she clambered back onto her feet. 'You know it has long been company policy that spouses should not be brought onto the field. I do hope you haven't divulged any sensitive information, thereby breaching security.'

'Of course I haven't,' Dan said, equally ignoring Beth. 'I had no idea she was going to come out here. This is as much of a surprise to me as it is to you.'

Tamara sniffed and looked down her nose at Beth. She looked to be in her early thirties, but had the attitude of an eccentric old woman living in a vast, deserted mansion that had been passed down the generations, of which she was the last one.

'We shall have to investigate, of course,' Tamara said. 'But not now. The contact is already on his way, and we need to hurry if you're going to meet him, as planned.'

'Yes, yes,' Dan said, and finally turned to look at Beth. 'I suppose it might be better if you went up to your room after all. You did book a room, didn't you?'

'I . . . yes . . . But wait . . . ' Beth's voice trailed off. She felt foolish and confused, and insignificant in the presence of this woman called Tamara. And was this really Dan, her husband of fifteen years, talking and acting like a complete stranger?

Dan grabbed a passing bellboy and spoke to him in rapid-fire French. The boy picked up Beth's suitcase and motioned to her to follow him.

'Dan?' Beth said.

But he was already striding away, across the cavernous foyer, with Tamara by his side.

★   ★   ★

Beth got as far as the elevator. The bellboy was pulling the black iron gate to one side, when she turned around just in time to catch Dan and Tamara leaving the hotel. Beth had no idea what Tamara had been talking about, but she was reasonably certain that Dan wasn't having an affair with her, after all. At least, Beth hoped not. Tamara was so frosty, Beth was surprised she hadn't caught a cold.

On a sudden impulse, Beth ran across the hotel foyer, leaving the puzzled bellboy holding her suitcase, and watching her go. Dodging an American couple, the woman carrying a small poodle in her arms, the man laughing loudly, she stepped outside and saw Dan and Tamara walking down the Rue de Renard. It was evening, but the city was ablaze with Christmas decorations, and the hotel windows glowed with warm, welcoming light. Beth felt a sudden ache in her chest. It was all so beautiful; and that should have been her walking down this Parisian street with Dan, not that cold, strident woman her husband was with right now.

Keeping a reasonable distance, Beth followed them. Tired from the flight over, and sick with anxiety and confusion, she felt she had no other option but to find out what was going on. Why was Dan with this horrible woman? Was she a colleague of his? And what on earth had got into her husband that he was acting in this strange way?

Normally he wouldn't say boo to a goose, and kept his head stuffed in a newspaper or a book. As far as Beth knew, he had no friends, no hobbies, no interests other than work. In fact, as she followed him through the Christmas crowds, examining his character in her mind, she began to wonder why she had ever married him.

He hadn't been like that at first, had he?

The man she remembered first meeting had been fun-loving and spontaneous, with an infectious laugh, and what seemed to be a permanent smile on his face. He held her hand, or wrapped an arm around her shoulders or her waist, and their friends joked that they were glued together. And if they weren't together, it seemed they spent all their time on the telephone chatting, or sometimes saying nothing at all, but reluctant to hang up and break the line between them. He bought her flowers and gifts of chocolate and perfume, and she hunted down copies of the books he loved so much, and allowed him to take her to see films that she had never heard of and had no interest in.

And they were in love.

Beth shivered and pulled her coat tighter around herself to ward out the cold.

How had their marriage come to this point, where she was following her husband, keeping at a distance, as he walked through the centre of Paris with another woman?

On the flight over, as they were preparing to land and the cabin crew were making sure everyone was buckled up, the pilot had said that there was snow forecast for later that evening. 'Looks like it might be a white Christmas after all,' he'd said, and Beth could believe it. Her breath billowed around her face in white streams, and there was a feeling in the air that the snow might start falling at any moment.

Tamara talked constantly as she walked, her hands gesticulating to emphasise important points, and Dan appeared to be listening intently, nodding his head occasionally but saying very little. It wasn't long before they left the main bustle of the wider city streets behind, and Beth had to hold back, widening the gap between them as there were less people to hide amongst.

Finally they stopped walking at a street corner beneath an old-fashioned street lamp casting an orange glow over them. Beth stepped into the shadow of a doorway, startling a black cat which bolted out and down the cobbled alley. The cat unnerved her, and Beth realised how silly she had been. She had absolutely no idea where she was, or how to get back to the hotel if she lost sight of Dan and Tamara.

They stood close together, talking

under the street lamp, and then Tamara left. Beth watched Dan check his watch, and then a moment later he walked off in the opposite direction to Tamara.

Beth was pleased the woman had left. She stepped out from the shadowed doorway and hurried after Dan. Now that he was on his own she was going to catch up with him, and demand to know what was going on.

And how to find her way back to the hotel.

She lost sight of her husband for a moment as he turned a corner. Picking up her pace, she reached the corner just in time to see him duck down another side street. Beth stifled feelings of unease, aware that if she let them grow she might end up panicking. This part of the city was much older, and less well-kept. There were no Christmas decorations, and only some of the street lights were working. As Beth ran down the cobbled street, she passed through pockets of dark and light.

An old man appeared out of the

shadows, a cigarette dangling from his lips, and muttered something to Beth. Startled, she ignored him and ran on, hearing him chuckling as she left him behind. When she got to the alleyway opening, Beth's worst fears were realised.

Dan was nowhere to be seen.

She was on her own now.

3

Beth sucked in a lungful of cold night air and held it.

Don't panic. Just keep calm, she thought.

Dan had to be close by; it was only a few moments before that she had lost sight of him. If she moved quickly, she should be able to find him.

But before she could do anything there was a noise behind her, and when she turned around she saw the old French man, the cigarette still dangling from his mouth, shuffling towards her. He was grinning, and nodding, and waving his hand at her.

Beth turned away and walked down the alleyway, hoping that he would leave her alone if she ignored him.

Where was Dan? He couldn't have gone far, surely.

Further down the narrow street was a

café with three small round tables surrounded by chairs set out the front, in defiance of the chill evening. Light blazed from the window, and Beth could hear the clink of cups and plates, and the gentle hum of conversation. Not daring to glance back to see if the old man was still shuffling after her, Beth headed for the café. Even if Dan wasn't there, at least she would be surrounded by other people, and she would be safe.

Peering through the partially steamed-up window, Beth could see the tiny café was full. A mixture of young and old, men and women, sat around tables draped in blue checked cloths, drinking coffee and eating baguettes and crêpes. Beth envied them their relaxed conversations and their happy, smiling faces. She suddenly felt very alone, and sad.

Her mood lifted when she saw Dan, sitting at a table towards the rear of the café with another man. They were huddled together, deep in conversation, and Dan hadn't spotted her. She lifted a hand to wave at him and get his attention, but then hesitated.

If he had been angry with her at the hotel, wouldn't he be even angrier when he saw her and realised that she had been following him? Beth didn't want to cause a scene in front of the café customers, didn't want to embarrass herself, but she needed to talk to Dan. There were so many questions whirling around in her mind.

Why was he acting so differently? What kind of government department did he work for, that they would pay for him to stay in expensive hotels in Paris? Why had he been so angry with her? And so dismissive?

And that woman, Tamara. Dan had never mentioned her before. But then he never spoke about anything to do with work. In fact, the more Beth thought about it, the more she realised she was completely clueless about how Dan spent his days in his job, whether he worked alone or with others, what the purpose of his work was, and why it took him away from home so often.

And really, had she ever questioned him that closely about it? Had she ever cared enough to find out more, as long as she saw the monthly wages coming into their shared bank account?

The sound of a bell tinkling broke into her thoughts. A man in a large overcoat, the collars pulled up, and a hat pulled low over his face, had opened the café door and stepped inside. Beth hadn't even been aware of him walking past her. Pushing aside her misgivings about how Dan would react when he saw her, she was about to follow the man into the café when she realised he had stopped in the doorway, blocking the entrance.

What she saw next took on the aspect of a slow-motion sequence in a movie. The man reached into his big overcoat and pulled out a gun. He held it out at arm's length, pointing it at Dan and the man he was talking to. Dan's companion had his back to the man in the café doorway, but Dan saw him, his eyes widening in shock. Before he had a chance to react, the man fired the gun, the sound of it a sharp crack, instantly silencing all the voices in the café.

Beth screamed, and the café erupted as chairs were pulled out and tables tipped over, the customers panicking and diving for the floor or charging to the rear of the café, looking for safety. Losing sight of Dan, not knowing if he was hurt or even alive, Beth rushed to the café doorway, not thinking for one moment about the fact that the man with the gun was still there.

He barrelled into her as he made his escape and they both fell and hit the ground, the cold cobblestones digging painfully into her side as the man landed on top of her. She caught a brief glimpse of his face: it was disconcertingly white and smooth, like a mask, or a mannequin's face. Beth closed her eyes and ground her teeth together, waiting for the sound of the gun firing again; waiting for this terrifying-looking man to shoot her.

But he didn't. A split second later he climbed off her, and she heard him running away.

'Beth?'

She opened her eyes. Dan was standing over her, his face white with shock.

'Oh my God, Beth, are you all right? Did he hurt you?'

'No, I'm fine,' she gasped. 'He just winded me.'

Dan knelt down and helped her sit up. 'Stay here. I'll be back as soon as I can.'

And then he was off, running down the cobblestoned street after the shooter.

Absolutely not, she thought as she clambered to her feet. *You're not leaving me alone again*.

Ignoring the sharp pain in her hip, she ran after her husband.

The alleyway opened out into a wider street with traffic. There was a sharp blaring of horns and the crunch of metal as someone crashed, followed by yells of protest. When Beth got to the end of the alley, she saw the man pulling a driver from his car and climbing inside. From the scene in front of her it looked as though he had simply stepped into the flow of traffic, causing an accident and an obstruction, so that he could grab himself a getaway vehicle. With an angry squeal of tyres, smoke pouring from the back wheels as they skidded against the tarmac, the car shot off.

Dan had pulled open the driver's door of another car — a rusty, ancient-looking 2cv6 — and spoke to the young man as he pulled him out of his seat.

'Dan, wait!' Beth shouted as she ran to him.

Dan looked at her, and she couldn't tell from his expression whether he was pleased to see her or angry.

'Oh for goodness' sake, hurry up and get in!' he shouted as he slammed the door shut.

Beth had hardly climbed into the passenger seat before he gunned the engine and they jerked forward.

'Fasten your seatbelt!' he shouted.

Beth pulled the strap over her shoulder and fumbled with the unfamiliar buckle.

'I always wondered what you did at work,' Beth said. 'Is this a typical day at the office for you, getting shot at and then stealing a car?'

'I haven't stolen this car, I've just borrowed it,' Dan replied.

'Oh, right,' Beth said, clinging to the dashboard as they skidded around a corner, the car lurching over to one side.

'Damn it, he's getting away,' Dan shouted.

'That's not a surprise, considering this car looks like it's held together with rust and spit,' she said, having to yell to make herself heard over the engine's scream as Dan tried to coax as much speed out of it as possible.

Beth wasn't sure what make or model the car up ahead was, but it was newer and faster than the 2cv6 they were rattling along in. If it hadn't been for the traffic on the roads, they would have lost the gunman by now. As it was, he had to keep swerving around other cars, his horn blaring as he tried to make an escape path.

Dan kept his foot down, the car rattling and shaking like a tin can rolling out of control down a hill. They both pitched violently from side to side as Dan swerved around other cars; and when he tried sounding the horn, its tinny little blare was barely audible above the scream of the engine.

'Look out!' Beth screamed as a car braked in front of them.

'Always criticising my driving, aren't you?' Dan shouted, spinning the steering wheel and narrowly avoiding a collision.

'I am not,' Beth replied, offended.

'Oh yes you are!' Dan punched the car horn again and gesticulated for someone to get out of his way, then put on a silly, nagging voice. ''You're driving too slowly, we'll never get there at this speed, do you have to put your handbrake on at *every* junction?''

They shot over a set of traffic lights on red, car horns blaring, and shouts of anger receding behind them.

'All right, I promise I will never nag you about stopping at junctions and putting the handbrake on ever again!' Beth said, gripping the edge of the dashboard even harder.

'Oh, so now I'm driving too fast, am I?'

Beth craned her head to look for the car they were pursuing.

'Maybe not fast enough; you're losing him.'

Dan sighed, and with a shake of his head changed down a gear, spun the steering wheel, and drove onto the pavement. Pedestrians dove out of the way as he hurtled past shops, scattering displays of books and tourist mementos, and Christmas decorations. Beth screamed as a model of the Eiffel Tower hurtled towards her and slammed into the windscreen, a spider's web of cracks instantly obscuring her view.

'We've got him now!' Dan yelled.

He was looking out of his side window at the red car braking to a halt, unable to swerve around a line of cars waiting at a junction.

Dan bounced the car off the pavement and onto the main road at the traffic lights, and Beth screamed as she saw another car heading straight for them.

A split second later, her world disappeared in a roar of twisting metal and shattering glass.

4

'Your husband is fine,' the young doctor said.

Beth was struggling to understand him a little, but at least he could speak English. Why had she thought she could come to France all on her own when she couldn't speak a word of the language?

Because she hadn't expected to be on her own, or end up in hospital.

They were sitting in a small side room with easy chairs and a coffee table, a water cooler, and a television in the corner. The news was on the TV, and the shot was of Notre Dame Cathedral in Paris. World political leaders had already been in Paris for a peace summit this last week, and were apparently finishing the summit on Christmas Eve with a carol service in the Notre Dame cathedral. The news report seemed to be about the security preparations taking place.

Beth had been watching the TV while waiting for the doctor to come and see her, concentrating hard on trying to understand what the news presenters were saying in an attempt to take her mind off Dan, who had been rushed unconscious into the hospital's emergency department. Beth had escaped the accident with a few bruises to her chest and stomach where the seatbelt had bit into her at the moment of the collision. But Dan, who had not been wearing a seatbelt, had smacked his head on the windscreen and been knocked out.

Waiting for the ambulance to arrive, holding Dan's limp hand had been the worst moments of Beth's life.

'Can he be discharged?' Beth asked.

'*Non*,' the young doctor said. 'He has suffered a . . . a concussion, and we need to keep him in overnight for observation.'

Beth and Dan had both been very

lucky to escape the car crash with their lives. The oncoming car had ploughed into the side of the Citroën, shoving them into the path of more traffic. Within moments the junction had become snarled up, the wreckage of the 2cv6 sitting in the middle. Fortunately the driver of the other car had only suffered minor injuries.

'Can I see him?' Beth said.

'Of course.' The doctor looked down and Beth's heart sank. He had something else he hadn't told her, some piece of bad news he was holding back. 'There is just one more thing.'

'What? What is it?'

'Your husband . . . the blow to his head has made him temporarily forgetful.'

'Forgetful?'

'He has . . . hmm, the English word, I am not sure . . . amnesia?'

'You mean he can't remember the accident?'

The doctor smiled sympathetically. 'I am afraid it is more than that. He cannot remember who he is, or why he is in Paris, or why he was driving somebody else's car. He can remember nothing.'

Beth bit her lip, resisting the urge to cry.

The doctor placed a gentle hand on her shoulder. 'Do not worry. In most cases like this, his memory will return. Probably in bits and pieces at first, and then in more of a rush. Give him a day or two and you'll see.'

Beth dabbed at her eyes, struggling to keep her emotions in check. 'This was all meant to be a lovely surprise for him. We were going to have a romantic Christmas in Paris.'

The doctor smiled sympathetically. 'You can come and see him now.'

He led Beth through to Dan's private room. Dan was sitting up in bed, gazing sleepily out of the window. He had a nasty-looking swollen bruise on his left temple, and his left eye was slightly swollen shut and bloodshot.

Beth pulled herself together, thanking the doctor as he left them alone.

'Hey,' she said. 'How are you feeling?'

Dan slowly turned his head to look at her. His eyes were hooded and dark with all the painkilling drugs they had given him.

'It's starting to snow,' he said, and returned to looking out of the window.

Beth took his hand and looked out of the window, too. The falling snow glittered against the dark of the night and the city lights.

'On the weather forecast they said it's going to be a white Christmas,' Beth said.

Dan looked down at Beth's hand holding his, and then up at her, and smiled. 'This is lovely,' he said.

Beth's heart skipped a beat. He could remember! He knew who she was!

'Do all the nurses in France take time to hold their patients' hands?' Dan said.

Beth swallowed the urge to cry and took a moment to compose herself. 'I'm not a nurse, Dan. I'm Beth, your wife.'

Dan's smile faded and his eyebrows

scrunched up in puzzlement. 'Really? I don't remember having a wife. Are you sure?'

Beth nodded. 'I'm sure. We've been married over fifteen years and we've got two children, Sophie and Toby.'

'Oh.' Dan pulled his hand away and looked out of the window again. 'I really don't remember any of that.'

'What *can* you remember?' Beth said.

'Tomato peel,' Dan said.

Trembling slightly, Beth took his hand again. To her relief, he didn't pull away. 'What do you mean, Dan? Tomato peel?'

'I don't know what it means. I can't remember anything, except those two words. Tomato peel.'

'Hey, buddy, how's it going?'

Beth twisted in her seat at the sound of the loud American voice. The big voice was accompanied by a big man filling the doorway, a huge grin on his face, his hands held out like he was doing an impersonation of the Fonz, and going, 'Heyyyy!'

Dan gazed at him sleepily and said,

'I'm not sure to be honest. I suppose you're my brother, are you?'

'Nah, I'm your twin sister,' he said, and bellowed with laughter.

'Who are you, really?' Beth said.

'I work with Dan,' he said, entering further into the room. 'Come on, buddy, what's up? You look like you've just picked yourself up off the floor after a night spent drinking Black Sambucas.'

Dan's grip on Beth's hand tightened slightly. 'I'm sorry, but I don't know who you are,' he said.

'We were in an accident, and Dan had a bump to the head, and he lost his memory,' Beth explained.

'Holy moly, brother, is that right?' The big man bent down, hands on his knees, and peered into Dan's eyes. 'You don't know your old drinking buddy at all?'

Dan gazed back at him, eyelids drooping, not even a flicker of recognition passing across his face.

The big man straightened up and stuck out a meaty hand for Beth to shake. 'My name's Parker. Peter Parker, like the wall crawler Spider-Man, you know. But everyone just calls me Parker.'

'Pleased to meet you, I suppose,' Beth said, offering her hand, which was engulfed by Parker's. She braced herself for a bone-crushing grip, but he was surprisingly gentle and shook her hand just once before letting go.

'It could have been under better circumstances, but I'm pleased to meet you, too, Beth. Dan's told me all about you.'

'He has?'

'Oh yeah, he's always gabbing on about you and the kids. Sophie and Toby, right?'

'That's right,' Beth said, and glanced at Dan, who had lain his head back against the pillow, his eyes slowly closing.

'Maybe we should leave the poor guy to get some sleep,' Parker whispered. 'He's not making much sense right now, is he?'

'No,' Beth replied. 'I think it must be

a combination of the after-effects of the concussion and the drugs they've given him.'

They stepped outside Dan's room.

'Can he remember anything at all?' Parker said, his voice low.

'It doesn't seem like it,' Beth said, suddenly tearing up again. 'He can't even remember who I am.'

Parker placed a big hand on her shoulder. 'Hey now, don't worry. He'll get his memory back, I'm sure.'

Beth pulled a tissue out of a pocket and dabbed at her eyes. 'This was supposed to be a romantic break away. It's our wedding anniversary the day after tomorrow, but now look at us. It's not going to be much of an anniversary when my husband can't even remember marrying me!'

'Like I said, don't worry. A good night's sleep and he'll probably wake up remembering absolutely everything. You'll see.'

'Thank you,' Beth said. 'You're being very kind.'

Parker pulled a business card from his wallet. 'Look, I've got to go now, but I'll be back in the morning. My cell number's on there if you need me.' He handed her the card. 'Anytime in the night, you give me a call if you need me, okay? Like I said, I'll be back in the morning, and we can make arrangements to get you two back home in time for Christmas.'

'Thank you,' Beth said. 'That's very kind.'

Parker flipped her a casual salute, and grinned at her. 'No problemo. I'll see you tomorrow, Beth.'

As Parker walked away, whistling as he went, Beth studied the business card.

Peter Parker.

Sales Officer, Cartwell International Shipping.

Was this the company that Dan worked for? He had never mentioned the name, and all these years Beth had assumed he worked for the government. But why had she assumed that?

Where had their relationship gone so wrong that she was now not even sure of who her husband worked for, or what he did?

Beth tucked the card away. At least the American was a friendly face, and an English-speaking one at that, just when she needed one.

She entered Dan's room again and sat down. He was fast asleep, his face looking composed and more relaxed than she had seen him in a long time. She remembered the first time they met, at St David's University. They had both been late for their lectures, and had collided when running through the university's beautiful landscaped grounds. Their textbooks had gone flying, and landed in a muddled heap on the grass. They were both in such a hurry that after a rushed apology, they simply scooped up their books and raced away. It was about half an hour later, in the middle of her lecture, that Beth realised she had mistakenly picked up one of Dan's books and taken it with her.

That evening she found his room and returned his book, and he said the least he could do to thank her was buy her a drink at the university bar. One drink led to another, and the evening passed in a whirl of conversation and laughter. Beth had been immediately struck by his brooding good looks; and even then, on that first date, he had gazed at her in a way in which nobody else ever had. That look had awoken butterflies in her tummy, and made her giddy with delight. A week later he asked her out.

Beth sighed, once more struck by how the years had sped by.

A feeling of sadness and slight foreboding crept over her. They had been so happy once, so giggly and full of fun. Every day had seemed like a fresh adventure in their relationship, and it wasn't long before they were married, and then Beth was expecting their first child. Maybe they had got married too young. Maybe it had been too soon in their relationship for children. But for whatever reason, something had gone wrong in their marriage.

How could Dan have been so secretive about his job? And why had he embroiled himself in a car chase across Paris? Beth had never seen him drive so recklessly before. He was always such a careful driver; maddeningly so, sometimes.

When she saw Parker again in the morning, she would have to ask him about Dan's job. It was about time she found out what he actually did for a living. And she wasn't going to be fobbed off with talk about boring presentations on obscure statistical, scientific mumbo-jumbo. This time she would get a concrete, specific answer, if it was the last thing she did.

She sighed, and began drifting off to sleep herself.

★   ★   ★

Beth flinched and woke up suddenly. For a moment she struggled to clear the fog from her mind, feeling confused and slightly panicky. Where was she? Why was she sitting in this unfamiliar chair, in this strange room?

But then the mists cleared in her mind, and the memory of the car crash came flooding back. The hospital room was dark, lit only by the glow of light from the hospital corridor. Dan was still fast asleep, snoring softly. Beth stretched and sat up straighter.

'Good, you're awake at last,' a female voice said.

'Who's there?' Beth asked, the panic returning, flooding through her chest and stomach, setting her body on full alert.

'It's me, Tamara.' She stepped out of the shadows by the window, and into a pool of light from the hospital corridor. She looked as composed and beautiful as she had back at the hotel.

The panic subsided, to be replaced by a sharp pang of jealousy.

Tamara gazed at Dan, at his face. Beth could imagine what she was thinking: that he looked so handsome and relaxed when he was asleep, the cares of the world no longer etched into his face. Beth wondered if she had seen him like this before, perhaps sharing a bed at the Prince de Galles, or some other hotel somewhere else in the world. It seemed that Dan had a whole different life that Beth knew nothing of, and maybe Tamara was a part of that world.

Then Dan snorted and mumbled something about watching out for cow pats on dinner plates, and the moment was broken.

'I'm sorry I couldn't get here sooner, but security has been compromised,' Tamara whispered.

'Compromised? What are you talking about?'

Tamara turned to look at Beth. 'I forgot — you don't know anything, do you?'

'Why don't you tell me?' Beth replied, her tone of voice cold and sharp.

'You probably thought Dan worked

for a very boring, very minor government department specialising in dusty
documents and boring conferences, is
that right?'

'I did until today, when I was suddenly plunged into a James Bond movie.'

'Hmm, James Bond isn't that far off
the mark, to be honest,' Tamara said
thoughtfully.

'What do you mean?'

Tamara pulled up another chair and
perched on the edge of it, as though she
might need to jump to her feet any
moment. 'I mean, your husband is not
the man you thought he was. He's been
living a double life for many years now,
a secret life away from you and your
family.'

'He's been having an affair with you,
hasn't he?' Beth blurted out.

Tamara shook her head and chuckled
softly. 'You might soon begin to wish it
were that simple. No, Dan and I are
work colleagues, as he said. We both
know not to mix business with romance;
it would only lead to disaster.'

'Oh good,' said Beth, annoyed. 'I'm glad you feel that way, otherwise you'd have just hopped into bed with him, would you?'

'Don't be silly,' Tamara replied. 'He's not my type at all.'

'Well, that makes me feel a lot better,' Beth said sarcastically. The more time she spent with this odd woman, the less she liked her.

Tamara leaned in closer, her voice dropping. 'Your husband is a secret agent working for a highly secret British government department called Section 13.'

'What? Dan? I've never heard anything so ridiculous. He's far too boring and sensible to be a secret agent.'

'Really?' Tamara arched a perfect eyebrow. 'He wasn't very boring when he was driving the car earlier, was he?'

'You know about that?'

'Of course I do. It's my job to know.'

'Why should I believe you? What you're telling me is just so incredible, it's completely mad. I should speak to his manager in England. He'll explain everything.'

Tamara glanced both ways, as though someone might be lurking just within earshot. 'You need to be careful who you talk to. We have a mole in the ministry.'

'A mole?' Beth said, imagining a furry creature burrowing out of the ground and leaving a pile of soil behind.

'A double agent, a spy. He's been with us for years, collecting information, sending it to *them*.'

'Them? Who's them?'

'Terrorists.'

Silence filled the room, that word hanging between them like an unexploded bomb.

And then Dan snorted again and muttered something about not saddling the cat up because he hadn't been oiled yet.

'Terrorists,' Beth whispered. 'What, you mean like — ?'

Tamara shook her head. 'No, worse. These terrorists are an amalgamation of

59

nationalities and cultures, but they are part of a new religion, with a single aim in mind. Unfortunately, that aim is not a peaceful one. They are dedicated to wiping out mainstream religions, decimating them in fact, until theirs is the only one left.'

'But what has any of that got to do with Dan?'

'Dan was meeting with a contact earlier tonight.'

'The man in the café!' Beth exclaimed, and then shot a quick glance at Dan to see if she had woken him. He was still fast asleep.

'That's right. You were there, weren't you?'

'Yes, I was standing looking through the window when a man walked past me and pulled out a gun and fired into the café.' Beth shuddered at the memory. 'When he ran outside he collided with me, and I got a brief look at his face. It was horrible, all white and plastic-looking, like he was wearing a mask.'

'The Ghost,' Tamara said. 'If he is

here in Paris we are in more trouble than I realised.'

A cold chill settled over Beth's heart and sank down into her stomach. She absolutely did not want to ask her next question, but she knew she couldn't stop herself.

'Who is the Ghost?'

'He is a contract killer. They call him the Ghost because of the way he looks. After every job he used to have plastic surgery to change his appearance, but the last time it went wrong, and now his facial muscles are frozen and his skin is bleached of melanin, giving him the look of a shop dummy. If he is the one who shot and killed our man in the café, that means the Order of Omicron have hired him to do their dirty work. We were hoping that our man would be passing on information to Dan tonight.' Tamara paused, looking thoughtful. 'The Order of Omicron, this religious cult, are planning something — a Christmas present, they have called it — for the people of the world. And we believe it's going to happen in Paris, and soon, but we have no details.'

'Oh my gosh,' Beth said. 'This is all so frightening and horrible.'

'Indeed,' Tamara replied, arching a perfect eyebrow. 'The problem is, they will know that Daniel was meeting with a double agent, and the likelihood is that the Ghost will be after you both now. They need to silence anyone who poses a threat to their plans, and that includes you two.'

'But why?'

'Because they don't know how much information Daniel was given in that café. They need to kill him as soon as possible before he passes it on.'

'This is awful,' Beth said. 'We should go to the police.'

'No!' Tamara snapped. 'That's the last thing you should do. Don't you understand? This is bigger than the police; this is a top-level security situation. What we need right now is for Daniel to wake up and tell us what he knows. We're hoping he was also told the name of the double agent in our organisation.'

Beth sagged back into the chair. 'Dan can't tell you anything; he's lost his memory. He can't even remember who I am, let alone what he does, or where he is, or how he ended up here. He couldn't even remember his friend who came by earlier.'

'Friend?' Tamara said. 'Who was this friend?'

'A big American man called Parker. Said he worked with Dan.'

'Peter Parker!' Tamara hissed. 'He has no business being here.'

'He stopped by to see how Dan is. He said he would be back in the morning to arrange our return home to England.'

'No, you mustn't go anywhere with him. I don't have any evidence, but I suspect Parker may be the double agent in our midst. In fact I have suspected him for years. The fact that he's here in Paris just confirms my suspicions.' She glanced at her watch. 'I have to go, but you need to be careful of Parker, he's a dangerous man. I'll be back in a couple of hours, and we'll get you both out the hospital before Parker returns.'

Tamara stood up and smoothed down her dress, and walked to the door.

'Wait!' Beth whispered. 'What do I do now? What about this assassin, the Ghost? And these people, this Order of . . .'

'Omicron. Don't worry, you're safe here for the moment. I have men stationed outside the hospital, keeping an eye on you both.'

'But how can I contact you?'

'You can't contact me,' Tamara replied. 'Wait here, and I'll be back soon.'

And with that she was gone.

5

When Beth awoke the following morning she was stiff and sore, and realised she had spent the whole night sleeping in the chair beside Dan's bed. Outside the hospital window the Paris streets were smothered in a deep blanket of pure white snow. The sky was heavy and grey, and looked ready to let loose another snowfall. In the distance Beth could see the Eiffel Tower, white against the gloomy sky.

'It's pretty, isn't it?' Dan said.

Beth started and turned around. Dan was standing behind her in his hospital gown, his hair mussed up, gazing out of the window. The bruise on his forehead looked a little better this morning.

'It's beautiful,' Beth said. 'Reminds me of the time we went to Austria, the year before we got married. Remember when we were in Innsbruck, walking through that churchyard, and everything was covered in fresh snow, just like today?'

Dan shifted his gaze from the view out of the window and smiled at Beth.

'And we were walking through the graveyard, and it was steep, and you slipped and fell over,' Beth continued. 'And there was a priest in his full black priest's outfit, and he laughed and laughed as he helped you up again.'

'No, I'm sorry, I don't remember any of that,' Dan said, his smile faltering. 'I wish I could; it sounds nice. Did we have a nice holiday?'

'It was one of the best,' Beth said, blinking away the tears. 'That was our last holiday before we got married, and before we had children. We travelled by train around Austria and stayed in youth hostels, and we spent all our time kissing and giggling and kissing some more, and we were like a pair of love-struck teenagers. One day we were sitting in a café, just gazing into each other's eyes, and we sat there so long we missed our train to Vienna. By the time we got to our hostel that we had booked, they had given our room to someone else, and we had to stay in this really grotty youth hostel where even the management partied all night long, and we didn't get a wink of sleep.' Beth sighed. 'We always intended to go back one day, because we never really saw much of the country; we were just so much in love, all we could do was look at each other.'

'Did we go back?'

Beth shook her head. 'No, not yet.'

They fell into a silence, both looking out of the window at the snow. Beth's heart ached at the thought that Dan had lost all his memories of their good times together, of the love they once had for each other, and their children. But then, thinking about the distance between them these last years, she couldn't help but wonder if those memories had meant much to him, after all.

Did it matter that he could no longer

remember them? Perhaps, if he didn't love her anymore, that was what, in combination with the bump to his head, had brought on this memory loss?

And if that was the case, what would happen when his memory did return?

Was it possible that he might decide to leave her?

Beth pushed that thought away, burying it deep inside where she could ignore it for the time being.

'Your colleague was here last night,' Beth said. 'Tamara.'

'Tomato peel,' Dan said.

'What? Why do you keep saying that — what does it mean?'

Dan's eyes focused back on Beth. 'That's what we call her. That's her nickname, Tomato Peel. Tamara Peel.'

'You remembered something!' Beth said, a flicker of excitement, mixed with apprehension, in her stomach. She took his hand and squeezed it. 'Dan, that's wonderful, you remembered something!'

Dan's face clouded over again.

'That's all I can remember, though. Tomato Peel. Not much is it?'

'No, but it's something. You'll remember more with time, I'm positive.'

'What did she say?'

Beth paused, hesitating to repeat what Tamara had told her. It all seemed so far-fetched, so utterly ridiculous.

'She said that you are a secret agent, that you work for the government, and that there's a double agent after you who's working for the enemy.'

'Wow,' Dan said, a flicker of a smile crossing his face. 'Sounds crazy, but exciting. Are you a secret agent, too?'

Beth huffed. 'No. I'm the boring stay-at-home mum.'

She then proceeded to tell him everything Tamara had told her about the Order of Omicron and the suspected terrorist attack they were plotting in Paris. Dan's face clouded over, any hint of amusement disappearing as she talked.

Dan scrunched his eyebrows up in an expression that Beth was very familiar with. He was mulling over what she had told him, and she knew better than to say anything and disturb his train of thought.

'I wish I could remember just something besides Tomato Peel.'

'We can find out more when she comes to collect us this morning. She should be here any time now.'

'You know what?' Dan said, his expression clearing. 'I'm going to get dressed. Whether I'm a secret agent or not, I have the feeling we should get going.'

'What do you mean?'

'I don't know, I can't explain it, but I think we should leave the hospital and find somewhere to stay while we think this through.'

'But Tomato . . . I mean Tamara, said we should stay here; that we should wait for her. And she said there were men stationed outside the hospital; that they were keeping us under close protection.'

'No, we should leave,' Dan said, his voice firm, and indicating there was no more room for discussion on the matter. 'I don't know how true any of this is, or if it is just one big practical joke, but my instincts are screaming at me right now to get out of this place and find somewhere safe to go.'

'All right,' Beth said a little uncertainly. 'If that's what you think is best.'

Dan opened up his locker and found his suit. 'Wow, nice clothes. Were we going to a posh party when we had the crash?'

'Um, no, not really.'

Dan lay his suit on the bed and looked at Beth. 'I'm sorry, but would you mind leaving the room whilst I get dressed?'

'Are you serious? Dan, I'm your wife, I've seen you without clothes on plenty of times!'

'I know. It's just that I can't remember any of that, and I don't really want to get undressed in front of a — '

'A stranger,' Beth finished for him, an ache of sadness suddenly blossoming in her chest.

She had come all the way to Paris because she was scared that she and

Dan had become strangers to each other. And now she was more of a stranger to him than ever before.

'All right, I'll wait outside,' she said sadly.

* * *

Back in his suit, Dan didn't look anywhere near as smart as he had last night. The jacket was creased and he hadn't bothered with the tie, leaving his shirt open at the collar. The young French doctor was on duty and tried to dissuade Dan from leaving before they had fully assessed him. Although Dan had lost his memory, he could still speak French, and quickly convinced the doctor in his own language that he was fine and wished to discharge himself. With a Gallic shrug, the doctor finally agreed.

They walked down the hospital corridor, a knot of tension growing in Beth's stomach. Was this really such a good idea? Leaving the hospital, with her husband who had lost his memory, who might or might not be a secret agent, with some very dangerous bad guys after him, in a foreign city with no knowledge of the language, and no idea where they were going?

Well, she had come out here with the intention of livening up their relationship. Surely it couldn't get much more exciting than this, even if it wasn't exactly what she'd had in mind.

At the other end of the corridor, the lift doors opened and Parker stepped out. He pulled up short as he noticed Beth and Dan walking towards him, his eyes widening in surprise.

'Hey, buddy, you're up and about! That's great!'

Dan grabbed Beth's arm and pulled him with her, pushing through a set of double doors.

'That's Parker, the one who said he works with you,' Beth said.

'I guessed as much,' Dan replied. 'But I don't trust him. Don't ask me why; I'm just running on instinct here.'

They were in another ward and

hurried past the nurses' station, past doors leading into side rooms and bays with patients lying in beds watching television or sleeping. No one took any notice of them, the nurses bustling by with trays of medication, carrying armfuls of patient notes, or talking with junior doctors.

Dan pushed through another set of double doors leading onto an adjacent ward. A sign on the wall, SORTIE, pointed down a corridor on their left.

'There's the way out,' Dan said, leading her down the corridor.

He kept up a fast-paced walk, constantly glancing back to see if Parker was following them.

'I think we lost him,' he said.

They found an elevator and Dan pushed the button to summon it. As they waited for it to rise from the ground floor, Beth watched her husband carefully. Was he really a secret agent? Or was he delusional because of the bump to his head? If it hadn't been for what Tamara had told her last night, and seeing Dan being

74

shot at in that café, Beth would have summoned a nurse to help her get him back to his bed, believing him to be mentally unstable due to the accident.

The elevator arrived and the doors opened. As they stepped inside, Parker rounded a corner further down the hospital corridor and spotted them.

'Hey, Beth! Dan! Wait up, will you?' He started running towards them and Dan hit the button for the ground floor.

'*S'il vous plaît tenir à l'écart des portes,*' the automated voice said.

'Come on, come on,' Dan muttered, staring at the open space in front of them, willing the elevator door to close.

'*Les portes se ferment,*' replied the automated voice.

Dan breathed a sigh of relief as the metal door slid into place. 'At last.'

As they began their descent, they heard Parker pounding on the door and his muffled voice fading away above them. On the ground floor, Dan took Beth's hand and hurried her through the exit. Outside the snow had started falling in thick, gentle flakes, but the roads and the pavements had been cleared.

They ran through the car park and down to the bus shelters, just as a bus pulled in. It was headed for the city centre, and they jumped on board, Dan supplying the language and Beth the money for the fare.

'Where are we going?' she asked as the bus left the hospital grounds.

'Into the city,' Dan said. 'After that, I'm not sure.'

'Maybe we should go back to the hotel, get your passport and luggage, and then head home.'

'Where's home?'

'England, Aylesbury.'

Beth went to take his hand, but Dan pulled away and looked out of the bus window. Beth clasped her hands together in her lap, telling herself to hold it together; that he wasn't himself right now.

'No, I don't think we should head back to the hotel just yet,' he said.

'Why not?'

'I don't know. I've just got this feeling

that it might be dangerous. I think we should find somewhere else to stay until I start remembering things again.'

Beth hesitated, not sure she should say what was on her mind. But she wanted to get it out in the open now, before she was thrown in too deep.

'What about me? If you can't remember anything, you don't know who I am either, so why should you trust me? I could be a double agent, too, couldn't I?'

Dan looked at her again, and a faint smile hovered on his lips. 'I don't know why I should trust you. You're absolutely right, you might be leading me into a trap. But somehow I get the feeling you're all right.'

He gets the feeling I'm all right, Beth thought. *Well, it's not exactly a passionate declaration of love, but it's something I suppose.*

★ ★ ★

They headed into the older quarter of Paris, where the streets were narrower, the buildings appearing to lean in on them as they walked, searching for somewhere to stay. They found a room over a small tavern that was decorated with twinkling fairy lights strung along the ancient wooden beams and exposed stonework. The old man, as wide as he was tall, and his tiny wife looked to be as ancient as the pub that they owned, but they were warm in their welcome and fussed over their two guests as though they were long-lost relatives.

In the squashed but homely room they were given, Beth looked uncomfortably at the four-poster double bed which filled the small space. It seemed to Beth that Dan's amnesia was starting to affect how she felt about him. That not only was she a stranger to him, but that he was now becoming a stranger to her.

'Maybe you'll have remembered who I am by tonight,' Beth suggested, breaking the silence that had grown between them as they stared at the bed.

'I'll sleep on the floor,' Dan said.

'Good luck finding a space,' Beth replied.

'Maybe I should book myself into another room.'

'Didn't she say this was the last one?'

'Maybe I should book myself into another hotel.'

'Now you sound like you want to get away from me.'

'It's not that, it's just — '

'I know, I know!' Beth snapped. 'I'm a stranger to you, and while I admire you for not sharing a bed at the drop of a hat with the first woman that you encounter who claims to be your wife, I'm still finding this situation incredibly difficult!'

The stress of the last twenty-four hours, the travelling, the argument with Dan in the hotel, the discovery that he wasn't who she had always believed him to be, the car crash, and his amnesia — it all suddenly caught up with Beth, and she burst into tears. She turned away from her husband and buried her face in her hands.

'Hey, I'm sorry,' Dan said, placing a gentle hand on her shoulder. 'Maybe we could sleep top to toe, how about that?'

Beth giggled between sobs and wiped the tears away with the heel of her hand. 'Absolutely not,' she said. 'There's no way you're putting those stinky feet of yours next to my head.'

'Charming, I must say.'

Beth looked at her husband, this man she had grown to know so well over the years of their relationship, and wondered what it must be like looking through his eyes and seeing a stranger who claimed to be his wife. But then, thinking about it now, she realised that Dan had become a stranger to her, too. After all, she knew nothing about his other life as a secret agent, working for a mysterious government department called Section 13.

Two strangers, sharing a room together.

'Hey,' Beth said softly, and took his hand. 'Maybe we should go on a date.'

Dan raised an eyebrow. Beth used to joke that he looked like Roger Moore when he did that. How ironic, considering the secret lark he had been keeping from her.

'A date?' he said.

'Yes, you know: a boy and a girl, they think they like each other, but they don't really know anything about the other person, so they decide to go out on a date.'

'Right.' Dan paused. 'Where do you want to go then?'

'How about we go downstairs to the bar?'

'All right.' He paused again. 'It's not going to be much of a date, considering I have no memory of who I am. I mean, I haven't exactly got a lot to tell you, have I?'

'Don't worry, I'll do all the talking.' Beth smiled. 'And I promise not to get you drunk and then drag you to bed.'

'Hmm. I'm not sure if I should be pleased or disappointed.'

'Steady, Tiger.'

Dan smiled, and it seemed to Beth that it had been years since she last saw him smile like that.

'I hope they have food downstairs, too,' he said. 'What was it your Auntie Cath used to say? 'I'm so hungry, I could gnaw my own arm off.''

'Dan — you remembered something!'

Dan's smile grew even wider. 'I did, didn't I?'

* * *

After eating a huge lunch downstairs, Beth and Dan went back to their room. Beth sat cross-legged on the bed, watching the snow fall through the tiny window set in the thick, uneven wall. Dan spent his time alternately pacing the tiny floor-space available to him, or sitting on the edge of the bed watching the snow fall with Beth. He had lit a fire, and the flames danced in the fireplace, the logs crackling and spitting.

'Tell me about us,' he said. 'Tell me

about our children.'

'Toby is twelve, and everyone says he is the spitting image of you. Everyone, that is, apart from you. You've always claimed he looks nothing like you, and for that you're grateful.'

'What does Toby think?'

'He's too busy playing on his Xbox or fighting with his sister to care about such minor things as his appearance.'

'Is he doing well at school?'

'Yes, despite the fact that he's not the least bit interested. Something else he shares in common with you, according to your mother.' Beth paused thoughtfully, watching the snow. 'Sophie is fourteen, and she takes after me in her looks, but you in most everything else.'

'Like what?'

'Like the way you hold yourself. When I saw you at the hotel yesterday, the way you were standing, the look on your face, you immediately reminded me of Sophie.'

'What about now?' Dan said, looking into Beth's eyes. 'Do I remind you of anyone right now?'

Beth looked at Dan and ran her fingertips gently down the side of his face, past the bruise on his forehead, and his eye, still slightly swollen from the accident. 'No. You're like a blank canvas waiting for the artist's first splash of colour, that first brush stroke.'

'That's how my mind feels,' he said. 'I look inside myself, try and examine my thoughts, and my head is like a big, empty room. I can run around it and search for something, some tiny scrap of memory — anything to tether myself to an identity — but there's nothing. Nothing at all.'

'Maybe you're trying too hard,' Beth whispered, still stroking his cheek. 'Why don't you close your eyes and let your mind go blank? Don't try to remember anything, just let your mind rest for a while.'

Dan closed his eyes. Beth took her hand away from his face, but he took hold of her wrist and guided it back, her palm against his cheek.

'Don't stop,' he said. 'That's nice.'

They sat in a comfortable silence, Beth reflecting that this was the longest they had spent together in ages.

Finally Dan stirred as though he was surfacing from a deep sleep, but he kept his eyes closed.

'What were you thinking about?' Beth whispered.

'Water,' Dan replied.

'Water?'

'Yes. I have an image in my mind of sitting up in bed one morning and being surrounded by water. Did our bedroom flood?'

'No, we were on holiday,' Beth said. 'This was before we were married. We went to Crete, and we woke up one morning to find our apartment had flooded. I remember you were so cross because your book was floating around the room, and it had swollen up to twice its size.'

'I remember!' Dan exclaimed. 'And didn't we get badly sunburnt that holiday?'

Beth giggled. 'You did, in particular. We had to spend two days indoors until the skin stopped peeling off your face. Even your eyelids were lobster-red.'

Dan smiled and opened his eyes.

They both twisted around on the bed as they heard the door opening behind them.

A large man stood in the doorway, filling it. He was wearing a large over-sized parka with fur trim around the hood, which had been pulled back off his head to reveal a white plastic-looking face.

Beth screamed, 'It's the Ghost!'

He stepped through the doorway, having to duck so as not to hit his head on the low frame, and shut the door behind him. He was holding a pistol, pointing it at Dan.

'Who are you?' Dan said, standing up and pulling Beth with him.

The Ghost said nothing. His mouth twitched as though he might be about to smile, or speak, but the flesh on his face looked stiff and hard. His eyes were small and held a deep black sheen to them, like obsidian.

Finally, his mouth opened in a strained, painful smile. A sharp pang of fear and revulsion shot through Beth as she realised that his teeth had been filed down to points, and were all studded with tiny diamonds.

The man raised the gun but, quicker than Beth had ever seen him move before, Dan crouched and grabbed the duvet, throwing it in his face. The Ghost recoiled as the duvet fell on top of him, and the gun went off, punching a hole through the duvet and setting off an explosion of feathers.

Beth ran for the door; but the assassin, still entangled beneath the duvet, fell against it, blocking her way. Dan grabbed the poker from the fireplace and swung it, hitting the man inside the duvet.

'Who are you?' he shouted. 'What do you want?'

The man's head appeared from beneath the duvet, and he bared his pointed teeth and growled at Dan, kicking and struggling against the blanket, against Dan's weight on top of him.

Beth yelped as someone pounded on their door.

'What's going on in there?' the landlord shouted. 'What's happening, what's all the noise?'

Distracted by the commotion, Dan looked away and his attacker took the chance to heave Dan off and grab a log from the hearth. He swung it, hitting Dan in the side of his upper arm. Dan grunted with the pain, dropping the poker and falling winded on the bed.

The man raised the thick log over his head, ready to smash it down on Dan's skull. Beth picked up an ornate vase with a pretty blue and white design, and threw it at the man's head. It smashed against his face and he rocked back in surprise, dropping the log on the floor.

Dan took his moment to launch a powerful kick at his attacker's stomach. He tumbled back, smashing through the window and outside. Beth ran to the window as the landlord used his pass key to open up, and burst into the room.

Beth looked down into the pretty snow-covered street, flakes of cold snow settling on her face and in her hair.

The Ghost was nowhere to be seen.

6

Watched by the landlord, his arms folded over his chest, Beth and Dan gathered their few possessions together and left the warmth and cosiness of their room — though with a cold breeze from the broken window making the fire splutter and flare, the room was becoming decidedly less warm and cosy by the second. All warmth was also distinctly absent from the landlord's manner, in contrast to his welcome. Beth couldn't blame him. She didn't imagine he had very many fights happening in his rooms.

They trooped downstairs, watched by the pub regulars as they were shown outside.

Where Tamara was waiting for them, with a car.

'I see you've had a spot of trouble,' she said.

Dan looked quizzically at Beth, his

eyebrows raised.

'Tomato Peel,' Beth whispered.

'I heard that!' Tamara snapped.

'Sorry,' Beth said. 'But it's the only thing he remembers.'

Tamara looked like she was sucking on a lemon. 'Well, that's something, I suppose.'

'Why are you here?' Dan said.

'I've come to collect you, take you somewhere safe.'

'Safe!' Dan exclaimed. 'You almost had us killed up there, and now you expect us to just get in your car so you can take us somewhere nice and quiet and get rid of us for good?'

'Dan?' Beth said, automatically reaching out and touching his arm.

'Don't be stupid, I'm on your side,' Tamara said.

Dan turned to Beth. 'It's just too convenient. That big gorilla up there with a face like a doll's tries to knock me into next week, and then when we come down here *she's* waiting for us!'

'That's ridiculous! Wait! What are you doing?'

91

Dan had grabbed Tamara and twisted her around, pushing her up against the car with her arms behind her back, like Beth had seen the police do on TV.

'Where are the keys?' Dan hissed.

'In the ignition,' Tamara gasped. 'Dan, please, you're making a big mistake.'

Dan let go of Tamara and pushed her away. He turned to Beth.

'Get in the car, quick. Tomato Peel's walking home from here. I'll bet she can find her way.'

'Dan, are you sure?'

'In the car, now!'

The car's interior was lovely and warm, and the seats were heated too. Dan got in the driver's side, and Beth watched Tamara standing all alone on the snowy street, looking after them as they drove away.

'The briefcase on the back seat,' Dan said. 'Grab it, take a look inside.'

Dan seemed to be a different person again. Authoritative, firm, a man of action. Beth could hardly believe what she had seen in their room — how Dan had sprung into instinctive action, fighting the intruder without a second thought. As though he had been trained in the art of combat and self-defence so thoroughly that even though he had amnesia, his fighting instincts still exploded into life when he was confronted with danger.

How long did it take for such training to become that ingrained in a person?

How many years had Dan been living this double life?

Since he changed his job?

Or had he already been a secret agent when they first met at university?

Beth twisted around and picked up the black briefcase. It was heavy and she struggled to get it into the front. There was a combination lock set into the briefcase, but when she pushed the sliders with her thumbs, each catch flipped open.

Beth gasped when she lifted the lid.

'It's full of money!'

Dan took a quick glance. He had switched on the headlights and was having to drive reasonably slowly through the swirling eddies of snow and the white roads.

'I knew it!' he said. 'That was obviously payment for having us eliminated. Tamara is the double agent, not Parker.'

'But Parker didn't even admit to being an agent. He was still pretending to me that you were simply work colleagues.'

'Maybe he was just trying to protect you, or maybe he *is* a double agent and had come to the hospital to kill me,' Dan said. 'I wish I could remember. Trying to work this out when I don't remember anything is impossible.'

'Where are we headed?' Beth said.

'Back to the hotel to pick up our passports and luggage, and then see if we can get out of Paris and go back home, or somewhere else maybe, somewhere safe.'

'Um, Dan?'

'Yes?'

'Can you even remember where the hotel is?'

'Oh,' Dan said, slowing the car down and turning to look at Beth. 'Can you?'

They had spent some time looking for the hotel when Dan stated that they were being followed.

'How can you tell?' Beth asked, twisting around in her seat to look out of the back window.

'What are you doing? Turn around again, before they realise we're on to them!'

Beth faced forward, feeling a combination of foolishness at possibly having given herself away, and anger at being spoken to like that.

'Well pardon me if my secret agent skills aren't up to scratch, but raising two children and making you a packed lunch for the last fifteen years hasn't exactly prepared me for a life of subterfuge!'

Dan turned a corner carefully, the back wheels spinning for a moment on the snow-covered road. 'We need to shake him off. Close that briefcase; we'll take it with us.'

Beth snapped the case shut. 'Are we stopping?'

'Yes, we'll be better off on foot. I can't lose him in the car in these conditions.'

Again, Beth thought of how Dan's instincts were driving his actions, despite the fact that he could remember nothing.

He pulled over to the side and they climbed out of the car. The sky was heavily overcast and visibility was poor, particularly through the heavy curtain of falling snow.

The red Lexus that had been following them skidded to a halt at an angle in front of their car, blocking any exit they might want to make. Beth recognised the American, Parker, climbing out of the car.

'Hey, Dan!' he shouted.

'Run!' Dan hissed, pushing Beth in the small of the back and almost sending her sprawling over the slippery pavement.

'Hey, buddy, wait up!' Parker shouted.

The street was filled with shoppers hurrying past, collars pulled up against the falling snow, a mass of colourful umbrellas bobbing above their heads. Beth dove into this crowd of people, clutching the briefcase, acutely aware of the large amount of money it contained. In amongst the throng Beth presumed they were hidden from view, but it was difficult to move. Women carrying plastic shopping bags stuffed with gifts, or pushing children's buggies laden with bright parcels, barged through, heedless of the cries of protests, or other shoppers.

Beth passed a Santa Claus ringing a bell and shouting '*Joyeux Noel!*' at the top of his voice. Music played from the open doors of the gift shops as she passed them, Bing Crosby singing 'White Christmas' from one, Bruce Springsteen shouting 'Santa Claus is coming to town' from another. The sights and sounds, the push of bodies and the snow all became a blur as Beth kept moving, fearful of a hand on her shoulder pulling her up short, or the muzzle of a gun in her back.

She risked a quick glance back, and pulled up short in horror.

Dan was no longer behind her. In their flight through the crush of bodies, they had become separated.

Someone bumped into her and cursed in French. At least it sounded like a curse, but Beth couldn't be entirely sure. Forced by the surge of shoppers into motion, she reluctantly began walking again, twisting her head and craning her neck as she sought out her husband in the crowd. It was an impossible task, with all these people, the umbrellas, the whirling snowflakes, and the colourful Christmas lights strung across the streets and over the shops combining to confuse her even more.

She turned a corner and found herself in a recessed courtyard. She stepped gratefully into it, out of the river of people flowing by. At the rear of the courtyard was the entrance to a museum of some kind, and a young couple stepped out of the doorway, arm in arm, foreheads touching, as they giggled and chatted. They looked so in love, and Beth's heart was pierced by a sudden pang of jealousy and sadness.

She envied them their youth and carefree attitude, and wanted to stop them and tell them to enjoy this moment, to savour it. Because before they knew it, they would turn around and in the blink of an eye find that the years had slipped by, the passion had gone from their relationship, they had children and responsibilities, and the humdrum reality of daily life had eroded their love for each other.

The couple slipped easily into the moving crowd of shoppers and, as they did, Beth spotted Parker. He stopped the young couple, quickly and easily conversing with them in French. Beth walked over to the museum entrance, hoping to hide in the shadows before he looked up and saw her.

'*Un billet pour une personne?*' a small bespectacled man behind the ticket desk asked.

'I'm sorry?' Beth mumbled, keeping an eye on Parker as he let the young couple go on their way.

'*Un billet est de dix euros s'il vous plaît,*' the man said.

Beth hunted in her purse for some money, once again conscious of the huge stash of euros she was carrying in the briefcase. Fumbling with the unfamiliar currency, Beth dropped some euros on the ground. She bent down to pick them up, and glanced through the door, into the courtyard.

Parker spotted her. He lifted a hand in greeting, and waved.

Beth shoved the money at the ticket man, and then quickly pushed her way through the turnstile. Hurrying through the small shop, selling books and post-cards, pens and notepads, and mugs, calendars, tea towels, and key rings with skulls attached to them, she stopped at the top of a stone spiral staircase.

Above the entrance was a sign: *Arrête! C'est ici l'empire de la Mort.*

Beth's French consisted of half-remembered words from her days at school, but she knew enough to recognise part of that sentence.

The Empire of Death.

Just what kind of museum was this?

Glancing back through the shop, between the displays, she could just see Parker arguing with the ticket man. There was no time to think about going back now. Taking a deep breath, Beth plunged through the doorway and began descending the ancient spiral staircase into the darkness, her way lit only by the flickering lamps on the walls.

7

The sound of Beth's shoes on the stone steps echoed around her as she hurried down into the darkness. She ran her hand along the stonework on her right, her fingers brushing over the damp, cool surface. The steps were not too narrow, but had been worn smooth from decades of visitors tramping up and down them, creating shallow indentations in the middle of each step.

The sound of her breath seemed to fill the small space, and her heart thumped in her chest from the exertion or fear; she wasn't sure.

At the bottom of the spiral staircase a chamber opened out. Beth paused. Somewhere, from an adjacent tunnel perhaps, she could hear the soft gurgling of running water. Was that faint laughter echoing up from the tunnel entrance on the opposite side of the chamber?

'Beth!' Parker's voice echoed down the spiral stairs. 'Beth, please wait! I'm only trying to help you!'

Could that be true? Tamara had said Parker was the double agent, but Dan believed she had set that thug upon them in their room. And why had she been carrying a briefcase stuffed with money?

But Parker had lied to her. He'd told her he was a colleague of Dan's. He'd mentioned nothing about being part of some governmental secret division.

But then hadn't Dan been lying to her all these years as well?

'Oh, Dan,' she whispered. 'Where are you? I need you. I don't know what to do.'

Clutching the briefcase, Beth strode across the uneven paved floor and entered the arched tunnel. The walls, formed out of mortared stone, closed in on her, and the tunnel twisted and turned, seeming to switch back on itself at times. Although there were no forks in the path to choose from, Beth soon began to feel hopelessly lost.

She hurried on, cursing herself for

having chosen an underground cavern as her escape route from Parker, and knowing that she could only keep heading forward. If she turned back, she would collide with her pursuer. She could only hope that there were other people down here, and that she might meet someone who spoke English.

On and on she walked, sometimes stumbling over the uneven floor, for what seemed like an age. Finally, convinced she must have walked a mile or more through the twisting tunnel, she entered another cavern. This one looked to have been quarried out of the earth, the space carved open rather than built with bricks or stone. In places Beth could see the roof had been reinforced, and occasional gaps in the rough walls had been bricked up.

In a recess at the far end of the cavern a model of a fortress had been carved out of the soft ground, including steps and pillars and fortified walls. A sign attached to a barrier separating visitors from it said that it was the

Port-Mahon Fortress.

Now Beth had a choice of two tunnel entrances to take. She faltered, indecision paralysing her.

How far behind was Parker? If she didn't get moving soon, he would catch up with her.

Another thought struck Beth. What if it wasn't pure chance that Parker was chasing her, rather than Dan? Surely he would have been able to see both of them; would have seen them get separated by the crowd. Why hadn't he chased Dan, who was surely of more importance to him than Beth?

Was it because she was carrying the briefcase?

Did Parker know what was in the briefcase?

Maybe it wasn't Beth he was after, but the money.

Beth lay the briefcase on the floor and snapped the locks undone. The harsh sound echoed around the underground cavern and she paused, listening whilst the noise faded. And then she heard the footsteps on the stone stairs, making their steady way down to her.

Looking at the stacks of money in the briefcase illuminated by the yellow glow of the electric lamps bolted to the walls, Beth picked up a wad of notes held together by an elastic band and shoved it in a pocket. Just in case she ran out of her own money. She could always pay it back at a later date. Then she stood up, quickly made her choice, and ran down one of the tunnel openings, leaving the briefcase of money behind.

If the cash was what Parker wanted, he was welcome to it.

The sound of her footsteps accompanied her through the dank, cold tunnel, echoing around her in the twisting, confined space. Beth felt trapped, weighed down by the Paris streets above, the buildings and the cars and the people. How could the city support itself when it was riddled with tunnels beneath its foundations?

Another thought struck Beth as she ran. What if she got lost down here?

Who knew how many openings she would come across, how many choices she would have to make about direction? Even if she escaped from Parker, would she be able to find her way back out again to the surface?

Beth stopped running and turned around. Maybe she should head back while she could still remember the route out. After all, Parker might have taken the other catacomb entrance.

But then his voice came hissing through the tunnel to her. 'Beth! Don't run — I want to help you!'

Beth turned and ran again.

Surely he would have seen the money in the briefcase? If he was still after her, then he had only one purpose in mind.

He was going to kill her.

The tunnel opened out into a chamber, and Beth pulled up short and screamed at the sight which met her.

The walls were lined with skulls. Empty eye sockets stared at her from every direction, rows and rows of human skulls embedded into the round chamber's walls. What kind of museum was this?

An empire of death.

Beth ran down another tunnel, having to stoop to avoid bashing her head on the ceiling. But now the walls of the tunnel were made of skulls and bones, rib cages, femurs and tibias, as if the labyrinth had been carved out of a huge cemetery. Her feet splashed through cold puddles as she ran. When she slipped once, Beth reached out a hand to steady herself. Her fingers slipped over a grimy skull and she screamed, the high-pitched sound of her voice echoing and taunting her as it faded away.

Hurrying down another passage, Beth wondered why she hadn't seen anybody else. Where were all the tourists? Somebody who could help her, protect her from Parker?

Not for the first time, she wished desperately that she had not become separated from Dan.

Beth stopped running, and gasped for breath. The way was blocked by a rusty iron gate, padlocked closed. Beth's fingers curled around the cold damp bars and she shook the gate in frustration. Even if it had been open she could not have gone any further. The electric lights were strung against the wall where it met the ceiling, stopped by the gate, and the tunnel disappeared into inky blackness.

Beth turned and started inching her way back, listening out for any signs of pursuit. Hundreds of skulls stared at her accusingly wherever she looked. She wanted to close her eyes and scream. She felt like she was in a nightmarish horror movie with no end.

She stopped walking and held her breath. Convinced she had heard foot-steps, she stayed rock-still, listening. The drip of water echoed through the tunnel, and again she could hear what sounded like a stream gurgling away somewhere. But no footsteps. Had she imagined it?

She started walking again, inching her way sideways through the tunnel, her back brushing the skeletons buried into the walls. At any moment she imagined the dead coming to life and a bony hand reaching out and taking her by the shoulder.

'Beth!' a voice hissed.

Beth! Beth! Beth! echoed the voice.

It was him.

Parker.

Suddenly the lights flickered and then went out, plunging Beth into a dank, clammy darkness. She held her breath, trying to keep the scream inside, scared that if she let it explode from her chest she would not stop screaming.

What had happened? Was it a power failure? Would there be somebody coming down to rescue them? How would she ever find her way out? Beth imagined herself lost down in the darkness of these tunnels beneath Paris, surrounded by skeletons, forever.

And what if there were rats down here? She shuddered as she imagined them scurrying across her feet, their repugnant squeaking filling her ears, their claws on her legs, and their teeth nibbling at her.

A hand grabbed her arm, the cold fingers closing around her wrist, gripping her tight. Her nightmares were coming true; the skeletons were coming to life, gathering themselves up, hundreds of skeletal arms reaching out for her, bony fingers grasping at her hair and face.

Beth screamed just as the lights flickered back into life.

'Hey, calm down, Beth. It's me, Parker.'

Beth sank against the wall, the scream dying in her throat. Forgetting all other concerns for the moment, she was simply grateful to see another human being.

The big American let go of her arm. 'I'm sorry, I didn't mean to scare you,' he said. 'I could hear you hyperventilating in the darkness, and I was just trying to get to you and reassure you. These lights go out all the time; they should provide everyone with a flashlight down here.'

'I was so scared,' Beth said. 'All these skeletons, and those skulls staring at me, just unnerved me. And then, when

111

the lights went out . . . '

'I know,' Parker said, and chuckled. 'Gave me quite a fright, too. To be honest, another few seconds in the dark and I think I would have been screaming a duet with you.'

Beth noticed the briefcase lying on the floor behind him. Her unease began pushing the relief away as she remembered why she was down here in the first place. That she had been trying to escape from this man.

Parker followed her gaze. 'You know, you should be more careful. That kind of money, you don't want to go leaving it around. Somebody's just gonna come and pick it up and take it home.'

'I thought you wanted it,' Beth said.

Parker shook his head. 'Nah. I wanted you.'

Beth stiffened, wondering what he was going to do.

'Don't look so scared. I'm not going to hurt you. I came after you to help you.'

'But you lied to me. You told me you

were a colleague of Dan's.'

'I am. Me and Dan, we've worked together for years.'

'But you didn't tell me he's a secret agent.'

Parker chuckled. 'Well, that's kind of the point, y'know. I wouldn't be much of a secret agent if I went around telling everyone, now, would I?'

Beth pulled herself away from the wall of skeletons.

'But Tamara, she said you're a double agent — that you work for some kind of extreme religious group.'

'She's lying,' Parker said. 'Tamara's the double agent. She's the one who set that thug everyone calls the Ghost on you earlier. I followed her there; I saw them talking. The money in that briefcase? That was for him, once he'd taken Dan out. Permanently.'

Beth shuddered. 'Why should I believe you?'

Parker extended his arms, hands out, and lifted his shoulders, a goofy grin on his face.

'Because I'm going to get you out of this underground horror chamber, take you to the nearest café, and buy you a hot cup of coffee?'

A flicker of a smile passed over Beth's face.

'Well, I suppose I could let you do that while you tell me more about who you are and what you do.'

8

Dan was lost. Not just lost in the physical sense in this strange foreign city, but lost inside his own mind, too. Somewhere behind all the fog that was clouding up his brain right now was a vague memory of something he needed to do. Something urgent and important. Maybe even life-or-death important.

But whenever he thought that memory might just be in his grasp, he tried reaching out for it, and it disappeared back into the fog. He had a feeling that someone told him once that when trying to remember something, a thought that danced on the outer edges of memory, you should relax, let your mind wander, and think about something else. That way the errant thought would creep back into your consciousness, and you could leap on it and pin it to the ground before it escaped.

But as much as Dan tried this, he couldn't help returning to circling this phantom idea that taunted him with its closeness but ran whenever he attempted to catch it. He had been told something of utmost importance; but whatever it was, it continued to elude him.

Dan slipped into an empty doorway, watching the Christmas shoppers passing him by. They were like two herds of cows heading in opposite directions, and they had become entangled with one another as they pushed their way onward.

Some instinct told him to stop running, to wait a moment and calm down. He had been so intent on losing Parker that he had managed to lose Beth, too. He had then spent the last ten minutes searching for her, but without success. If he wasn't careful they could become hopelessly separated, and he wasn't sure they would be able to find each other again.

He just wished he could remember something, anything, that might help him out in this situation. What Beth said, could it be true? Was he really a secret agent for the British government? It seemed quite likely, considering the fighting instincts he had automatically displayed when that man called the Ghost attacked him in their room. Dan's mind and body had gone into autopilot, as though somebody else was in charge, and the fog had cleared from his mind to be replaced by the ice-cold intent to protect Beth and himself from the threat.

And again, when they got outside and were met by the woman called Tamara Peel, Dan's instincts had been not to trust her. Now that he examined that thought, he was sure it wasn't because he knew or suspected anything about that woman. It was simply that he had been trained not to trust anyone until he knew otherwise.

Except Beth.

Somehow his defences crumbled and fell whenever he looked at the woman who claimed to be his wife, and he had no choice other than to put his trust in her. Whenever he looked at her, whenever she spoke to him, touched his hand, something shifted inside him. And the way she looked at him, those eyes, so intense, he sometimes felt that if he met her gaze for long enough the memories would come rushing back.

That she was telling the truth about their marriage, he was confident; but along with the rest of his life, he had no memory of Beth or the years they had spent together.

Apart from little fragments of memory, images really, that floated in and out of his mind. They were appearing for no reason at all, and then disappearing just as quickly.

Reclining in a deck chair in a garden, the sun warm on his face and a cat prowling around his feet. He could hear children laughing and whooping, and although he couldn't see them, he had an idea they were on a trampoline.

Climbing reluctantly out of bed, in the darkness of a winter's morning. It's early, and Beth is still asleep, and Dan feels strangely guilty at this memory, as though he feels he should be there when she wakes up, but knows he won't be.

Holding a little girl's hand, and is this his daughter? It is her first day at school, but Dan can't remember any more.

The memories came and went. They were gossamer-thin, and held so little substance that Dan wasn't sure if they were real or not.

And could it be true that he had lived the life of a secret agent, without his wife ever knowing about it, or even suspecting something?

Dan balled his fists up in frustration, willing the memories to return, to solidify and become real, to give him hope that he would get his sense of self back. Right now, not only was everybody he met a stranger even if they claimed to be a friend, but he was a stranger in his own body. He wanted to scream and yell and pound his fists against the door behind him, and he was aware of his whole body tensing up, his heart rate increasing.

Dan closed his eyes.

Relax, empty your mind. You're working too hard to try and recover your memories, your life. Accept your situation for the moment — just be. If you keep chasing those thoughts they may run and escape completely, and then you will never remember.

Slowly the tension began dissipating, and he started feeling in control once more.

Opening his eyes, the first thing Dan saw was Parker leading Beth through the crowd of shoppers on the opposite side of the road.

He left the doorway and began following them.

★   ★   ★

Parker took Beth to the Café des Deux Moulins, its rounded frontage sitting on the corner of two cobblestone streets.

Bicycles were parked outside despite the weather, but the tables on the pavement were empty. Above the awning, the café name glowed softly in the dull daylight.

The interior looked vaguely familiar to Beth. The elegant curved coving ran around the ceiling, and there was a long line of tables with a cushioned bench down the length of the café on one side, and simple chairs opposite. There was a long bar, which served alcoholic drinks as well as coffees and teas. On the wall behind the bar was a large framed photograph of a young woman, dark hair cut in a short bob, taken in the café. She was gazing out of the picture, and she also looked familiar.

Parker bought them both a coffee and they sat at a table. 'You ever seen the movie *Amelie*?' he asked.

'I thought I recognised this café!' Beth said.

'Yeah, this is where they made the film. Not only that, but the café is named after two windmills located nearby, one called Moulin de la Galette and the other one Moulin Rouge, another movie reference.'

Beth took a sip of her coffee, but it was hot and scalded her lip a little. She put the cup down.

'How did you enjoy your trip down into the Catacombs of Paris, then?' Parker chuckled.

'It was horrible,' Beth replied. 'What a nasty, gruesome place.'

'Originally those tunnels were limestone mines, built sometime after the 12th century. They got forgotten about, but when the city of Paris began extending out, people soon became aware of them again because buildings started collapsing and falling down holes that suddenly appeared out of nowhere. This was in the 18th century, and Louis XVI commissioned an investigation and exploration of the tunnel system. Turned out there are miles and miles of them, a labyrinth of passages and caverns, forgotten about for hundreds of years. That's why, apart from the Eiffel Tower, you won't find many tall buildings in Paris. The foundations just aren't there to support them.'

'But what about all the skulls, and the skeletons?'

'About the time the king had ordered an investigation into the tunnels, the Parisian cemeteries were full to overflowing. It was decided to exhume all the bodies and line the walls of the catacombs with the skeletons, as a kind of memorial to the dead.'

'And then they turned it into a tourist attraction?'

Parker laughed. 'Yeah, that's the French for you, I guess.'

Beth found it strange to think that only a short while ago she had been running away from this man, and now she was sat drinking coffee with him. She was growing increasingly relaxed in his presence, and she liked his easy laugh and friendly manner.

But still, she knew nothing about him. As far as she knew, he could be the double agent that Tamara had accused him of being, one of these . . . what had she called them? The Order of Omicron, that was it.

If only Dan was here, he would know what to do. Even if his mind was a blank slate at the moment.

'You're starting to look worried again,' Parker said, breaking into her thoughts.

Beth picked up her coffee and took another sip. It was still too hot to drink, but the action gave her a moment or two to compose her thoughts.

'Well, I was just thinking — you've bought me coffee, and you haven't tried bumping me off, or kidnapping me; but still, I don't know anything about you. Why should I trust you?'

'Good question,' Parker replied. 'That guy in your room, the one intending to blow holes in you both with that peashooter of his — did you notice anything about him?'

'Other than the fact that he was big and scary, and he was pointing a gun at us, no. I was too busy worrying about how we were going to stay alive.'

'Did you notice his face?'

Beth shuddered. 'Yes, it was horrible. He looked like a living, moving mannequin. And his teeth, too. They were all filed down to points.'

'And he had diamond studs in them, right?'

Beth nodded. She wasn't sure she would ever be able to forget the sight of the assassin called the Ghost.

'Those diamond studs? He had them inserted in the front face of each and every tooth in his mouth, at the same time as he had them filed down to sharp points. The way I've heard the story, he refused any anaesthetic, and let the dentist drill through his teeth and screw those studs in with no pain relief at all.'

'But what kind of dentist would be willing to do something like that?'

'The kind who works on the other side of the law, and enjoys the good life. He'd have been paid well for an operation like that. The point I'm trying to make is that this guy the Ghost is one mean mother. He enjoys inflicting pain on himself almost as much as he enjoys inflicting it on others.'

Beth shuddered again and took a sip of her coffee.

'And those teeth filed down to points? They're not just for show. Get close enough, and he'll sink those teeth into your arm or leg, or whatever body part happens to be handy.'

'Ugh, you make him sound like a zombie, or Hannibal Lecter.'

'Those are valid comparisons, except to say that the Ghost is far worse than either a zombie, or Lecter.'

'If you are trying to scare me, you're succeeding.'

'Good,' Parker said. 'You ought to be scared, you and Dan both.'

Beth took another sip of her coffee, Parker watching her. He seemed to be expecting her to say something, waiting perhaps for her to say that she believed him, trusted him. But there was just so much to take in, she was finding it difficult to process it all.

'Beth,' Parker said finally, 'we need to find Dan. These guys — the Order of Omicron and this assassin, the Ghost — they don't mess around. You and Dan are in terrible danger, and we should get you both to a safe house while we work out what it is they want and why they're in Paris. Have you any idea where he is?'

'No,' Beth replied, placing her cup back in its saucer. 'Dan thought you were trying to kill us. When we left the car we got split up in the crowds.'

'Damn. We need to get to him before the Ghost does, and then we need to get him to remember what our contact told him. The Order of Omicron have got something big planned for Christmas Eve — a Christmas present to the world they're calling it; only their idea of a Christmas present has nothing to do with peace on earth and goodwill to all men, but death and destruction on a massive scale.'

'But Christmas Eve is tomorrow!' Beth gasped.

'I know. Now can you understand the urgency of the situation?'

Parker looked grim and Beth shivered, thinking that the subject of their conversation was in stark contrast to the joyous trappings of Christmas decorations surrounding them.

'Have you any idea at all what they're planning?' she asked.

'The fact that they're here in Paris means it's got something to do with the international peace gathering the French President has been hosting. The Prime Minister is here, and the American President, too. By tomorrow morning half of the western world's leaders will be gathering in Paris, and later that afternoon they will all be in Notre Dame Cathedral for a carol service. That's most likely when the Order are planning to strike, but we have no idea how. We have to find out what they are plotting before they unleash a massive terrorist attack.'

Beth looked at her half-finished coffee. She had suddenly lost the taste for it, her stomach churning with fear.

From worrying about the state of her marriage, to now fearing for the safety of world peace, she could hardly believe this was happening to her. Surely she was dreaming. All she wanted to do was find Dan and return home to England, to her family.

Christmas in Paris had suddenly lost its appeal.

As if in counterpoint to their talk about terrorist attacks and world peace, the café door opened and a Father Christmas walked inside. Beth wondered if it was the same one she had seen earlier, when she was on the run from Parker. He had obviously got too cold standing outside, ringing his bell and shouting *Joyeux Noel*, and decided to come inside for a warm drink. He stamped his feet on the doormat and brushed snow off his red suit.

Beth jumped as her mobile phone started ringing. Looking apologetically at Parker, she said, 'I'm sorry, I'd better take this.'

'Hi, Beth!' her sister Sara said. She

sounded so clear and so close, it made Beth's heart ache to hear her voice.

'Hi, Sara,' she said.

'How is Paris? I hear it's snowing over there — how wonderful! And Dan, was he pleased to see you?'

Beth looked at Parker, wondering how much she could tell Sara. As if reading her mind, he shook his head and frowned.

'Paris is beautiful,' she said, looking out of the window at the snowflakes floating to the ground, blanketing the street and the shoppers in white. 'We're having a white Christmas here, and the city looks stunning.'

'Have you been up the Eiffel Tower yet?'

'No, not yet.'

'And Dan — I bet he was surprised to see you, wasn't he? Is everything all right between you guys?'

Beth looked at Parker again. He was still frowning, staring at her intently.

'Oh yes, he was very surprised,' Beth said. 'But pleased too. Everything's fine,

Sara, just like you said it would be.'

'Oh good, I'm so relieved. I've been worried about you two. Oh, hey, Toby and Sophie want to say hi.'

'Hi, Mum!' two voices chorused from the background.

Beth's ache deepened at the sound of her children's voices. All she wanted was to be back home with them, safe in the embrace of her family.

Beth noticed that the Father Christmas was drawing closer, weaving between the tables, drawing a few strange looks. Was he asking for money, or collecting for a charity, maybe? Parker hadn't noticed him yet, sitting with his back to him. It wasn't the Father Christmas she had seen earlier. This one looked a little tattier, his outfit frayed around the edges, his beard slightly grey rather than white.

'Oh, Mum, is it beautiful in Paris?' Sophie asked, her voice high with excitement.

'It's lovely,' Beth said. 'Are you two being good for Auntie Sara? You're not fighting, are you?'

'Mum, I'm fourteen years old! When are you going to stop treating me like a little girl?'

'I'm sorry,' Beth said, smiling a little despite the tension she felt. 'What about Toby?'

'Huh. Toby just spends all his time on the Xbox, playing Minecraft.'

Father Christmas was almost at their table; he was heading straight for them. Beth didn't like this. She had a feeling something bad was about to happen.

'Well, that's nice,' she said absently. 'I've got to go now, Sophie. Love you, missing you all, see you soon.'

She hung up before Sophie replied. Parker noticed that she was looking over his shoulder at something, and swivelled in his chair — too late. Father Christmas had bent down and wrapped his arm around Parker's neck. Parker reached up, pawing at the red suit, his back arched as he tried to relieve the pressure exerted on his windpipe.

'Relax,' Father Christmas said. 'I'm

not going to kill you.'

With his free hand he pulled back his hood and yanked his false beard down.

'Dan!' Beth gasped.

'Hey, buddy,' Parker croaked. 'Nice outfit. We were wondering where you'd got to.'

Some of the café customers had stood up, aware of the commotion, staring at Dan and Parker. Dan let go of Parker and clapped him on the shoulder, looking at the other customers and laughing. 'It's okay, we're friends,' he said in French. 'Just a practical joke, that's all.'

As everybody returned to their seats, chuckling and shaking their heads, Dan sat next to Parker and said in a low voice, 'Try anything, and I will not hesitate to kill you.'

'Dan!' Beth said, horrified.

Parker lifted his hands and chuckled. 'Don't worry, bud, you got me. You wanna grab a coffee and talk about this?'

'No, I want your car keys.'

'My what?'

'You heard me. Me and Beth, we're getting out of here, and you can't follow us if you don't have a car, can you?'

'But Dan, he's trying to help us,' Beth said. 'There's this terrorist group, and they're going to — '

'Don't believe a word he says, Beth. Right now, we can't trust anyone.'

'You'd better listen to her, Dan. She's right, there's some serious — '

'Shut up and hand me your car keys. Slowly.'

Parker reached into his pocket and pulled out a bunch of keys. He placed them on the table.

Dan scooped them up and glanced at Beth. 'Pick up the briefcase. We might need the money.'

Beth did as she was told. Once again Dan was acting like a stranger to her, so decisive and in control. It seemed like he was three different people: the man she had first met and fallen in love with, the husband who had grown more distant and cool as the years passed, and now this complete stranger who acted like he was in a James Bond movie and had no memory of his previous life. Would she ever be able to find the man she had first fallen for? Or was it too late for that? Maybe the man she had thought she had known and fallen in love with never existed. Perhaps Dan's whole life had been a lie, and Beth had been nothing but a convenient prop to help cover up his profession as a spy or secret agent, or whatever it was everyone claimed him to be.

They left the café, people at the tables looking at them once more, realising perhaps that something was not quite what it seemed after all. Beth glanced back. Parker had stood up, and he had his mobile phone to his ear. She wondered who he was calling.

Outside the snow was falling heavily. Dan held out the key fob, pointing it at Parker's car, and pressed the button.

Nothing happened.

'Come on, buddy!' Parker shouted,

standing in the doorway to the café. 'You didn't really think I'd given you the right key, did you?'

'Dan, when we left, he was phoning someone on his mobile,' Beth said.

Dan grabbed Beth's hand.

'Come on. Run!'

'Hey, buddy, I just want to help!' Parker shouted.

They hurtled down the street, slipping in the snow, barging through the crowds of last-minute Christmas shoppers. Although it was only the afternoon, it was growing dark and the Christmas lights were on, casting their multicoloured glow over everything. Dan gripped Beth's hand tightly, determined not to lose her this time. Heads turned and mouths opened as the shoppers watched the Father Christmas dash past them, pulling a woman behind him.

They arrived at a Metro station and flew down the steps.

Oh no, not underground again, Beth thought.

At the bottom of the stairs the station

was milling with people. There were a few French curses shouted as Dan pushed his way through the crowd. Beth risked a glance back and saw Parker forcing his way through the mass of people towards them.

'He's still behind us,' she said.

'I know,' Dan replied grimly. 'We'll lose him when we get on the train.'

'Can't you just talk to him? He might be trying to help us.'

'And he might have been calling someone like the Ghost to join in the chase. We can't trust anyone, Beth. Not until I can remember what's going on, and who I am.'

Dan pushed past a queue, elbowing people out of his way.

'Sorry! Sorry!' Beth said, as angry commuters and shoppers cast filthy glances at them and protested loudly. 'Dan, don't we need a ticket to get through the barrier?' she said as they pulled up in front of a turnstile.

'No time for that,' he replied, and jumped over the metal barrier.

'*Hé vous, que pensez-vous que vous faites?*' someone shouted as Dan helped Beth climb over the turnstile with the briefcase.

They ran down a brightly lit tunnel, the walls covered in colourful advertisements showing off glamorous couples drinking, or eating in a restaurant, or walking hand in hand along a sun-kissed beach.

And here Beth was, being dragged through the Paris Underground by a crazed-looking Father Christmas and carrying a briefcase full of money.

This wasn't the romantic Christmas break in Paris she had hoped for.

The tunnel opened out onto a crowded platform, a warm rush of air the sign that a train was approaching. Dan forced his way through to the front as the train shot out of the tunnel, then slowed dramatically with a whoosh of brakes. The doors opened and men, women and children spilled out onto the platform. The tannoy blared into life, a voice rattling off a list of the train's destinations, as the people behind Dan and Beth grumbled and jostled their way forward.

Beth and Dan got on the train. There were no seats left so they stood together, holding on to the handrail, waiting anxiously for the train to leave the station.

Slowly, Beth became aware of a pungent, vaguely unpleasant aroma. Leaning in towards Dan, she whispered, 'What's that smell?'

Her husband shifted uncomfortably. 'Um, it might be me.'

'You?'

An old man standing next to them looked Dan up and down, then did his best to move away, his nose wrinkling.

In the warmth of the train carriage, amongst the bodies packed together, the smell was getting worse. There was more than a hint of body odour, underlaid with an unmistakable whiff of kitchen bins, and topped off with the distinctive scent of pee. And now that Beth had a moment to examine the Father Christmas outfit, she realised it wasn't exactly clean.

'Where on earth did you get this costume?' she said.

'You really don't want to know,' replied Dan.

'Was it a homeless person?'

Dan nodded, looking slightly shame-faced.

'I don't believe it! How could you?'

'I needed a disguise so I could get close to you and rescue you from Parker!' Dan hissed, leaning in close.

Beth recoiled, trying not to breathe in. 'But even so, you stole clothes off a homeless man!'

'I didn't steal anything. We traded and, I have to say, he got the better end of the deal.'

'Oh no, what did you trade with him?'

Dan suddenly looked a little sheep-ish. 'My clothes.'

'Not that lovely suit?'

Dan nodded.

Beth hooked a finger over the collar of his red Father Christmas jacket and pulled it down slightly, to reveal the top of his chest.

'Are you wearing anything under there?'

Dan shook his head.

'Nothing at all?'

'Not a stitch. He wanted everything — pants, shoes and socks included.'

Beth looked down and noticed the tatty black boots for the first time. She covered her mouth with her hand and giggled.

'Well, I'm glad you find it funny,' Dan said, and hitched up the red trousers.

The train doors slid closed and the carriage jolted into motion.

'Looks like we lost Parker,' Beth said.

'I don't know,' Dan said quietly, staring intently out of the window onto the platform, until the train plunged into the dark tunnel. 'Maybe, maybe not.'

9

As the train hurtled through the tunnel, the carriage rattling and the passengers swaying gently, Beth quickly explained to Dan in a hushed voice everything that Parker had told her. Dan frowned as Beth talked, saying nothing and letting Beth tell her story. When they pulled into the next station, he hushed her and kept a lookout for Parker or any suspicious-looking characters boarding the train.

They left the light of the platform behind and plunged back into the dark tunnel. Beth shivered as she remembered the catacombs, the walls of skeletons and skulls peering at her with empty eye sockets.

'I just don't understand why Parker would tell me all of this if he was a double agent,' Beth said.

'Maybe he's using the truth to try

and draw me out where he can get me,' Dan said. 'Or maybe it's all a lie, a fantastic story to keep us both unnerved and on edge.'

'But Tamara said she suspected a terrorist plot, too.'

Dan hitched up his Father Christmas trousers and Beth suppressed a smile. They were obviously too big for him and in danger of slipping down around his ankles at any moment, which would be highly embarrassing considering he wasn't even wearing any pants. As soon as they could, they had to buy him some new clothes. Beth gripped the briefcase handle, the money inside like an unexploded bomb.

Well, at least they weren't short of spare cash.

Dan had his thoughtful look on, one she recognised from watching him struggle with a particularly difficult crossword, or sometimes when he brought work home with him and was poring over a thick wad of heavily typed documents. It was suddenly reassuring to recognise a part of him that she thought she had lost, and she caught her breath. All the worrying she had done over the last few months — about how far apart they had drifted, how they never spoke, and how she felt she didn't know who her husband was anymore — and now look at them.

Part of her was yearning for that husband of hers to return. It might be that he was distant and boring, quiet and unassuming; but at least she knew him, and he was a constant presence in her life. But then another part of her was enjoying the intrigue and the excitement. Dan might not be able to remember anything about their marriage, their relationship over the years, but they had spent more time together and spoken more in the last twenty-four hours than in the last few years, it seemed.

Beth had come out to Paris intending to inject some excitement into their marriage. This wasn't anywhere near what she had intended or imagined, but it was exciting and fun.

Sort of.

But even when Dan's memory returned, as the doctor had assured her it would, Beth had the feeling that her own little world had been permanently turned upside down, and nothing would ever be the same again.

'That was a big sigh,' Dan said, breaking into Beth's thoughts.

'Oh, sorry, I didn't even realise I had been sighing.'

'You looked very sad and thoughtful,' Dan replied, gazing down at her.

'I was just thinking about how this trip to Paris has turned out to be nothing like I expected or intended. I was going to take you to the Eiffel Tower, and we were going to go to the very top and kiss with Paris stretching out on all sides below us. Did you know it's our wedding anniversary on Christmas Eve?'

'No, I — '

'Of course you didn't,' Beth said. 'What a stupid thing for me to say, when you can't remember anything at all.'

Dan caressed her cheek with his

fingers. 'Don't be so hard on yourself. This must be incredibly difficult for you.'

Beth turned her head, looking at her vague reflection in the darkened window, and struggled to hold back the tears.

'What was I like as your husband?' Dan asked. 'Was I a good husband to you?'

Beth nodded. 'Yes — at first, anyway. We were very much in love and hardly ever apart. But then the years passed by, and the children arrived, and we just seemed to drift further and further away from each other.'

'Looking at you now, getting to know you all over again, I find that hard to believe,' Dan said.

Beth brushed a tear away, still unable to look at her husband. 'It was just that you were always working, or away so often. And you were always so mysterious about your job. Whenever I asked you about your day at work, or tried to show any kind of interest in what you did, you always fobbed me off with vague talk of statistics and boring conferences.'

'It doesn't sound as though I treated you very well,' Dan said.

He tucked a stray lock of hair behind Beth's ear, and she trembled a little at his touch. How long had it been since he last touched her in this way? Months? Years? How long since they had last shown each other any kind of affection, or said 'I love you'?

'Oh, don't go blaming yourself too much,' Beth said, and turned around to face Dan again. 'Maybe I played my own part, too. It is so easy to become sucked into the frantic pace of each and every day that I think we become blind to the passing of the years. It seems like only yesterday that Sophie was born, and now she's a teenager.'

'Was I there at the birth?'

Beth smiled. 'Yes, you were. I had a caesarean; I remember lying on the theatre bed while the surgeon stitched me up, and you sitting next to me, cradling Sophie in your arms. She was all wrapped up, and I could just see her tiny little face gazing up at you whilst you gazed back at her. And I remember looking at you and thinking, 'I have to share him now. He's not just my husband, but he's a father, too.''

Dan had been running his fingers through Beth's dark, wavy hair. He dropped his hand by his side and tipped his head back, as though seeking help from the heavens.

'I wish I could remember this. It's as though you are talking about another person, or as if someone has come and stolen my life away from me. I keep getting these little fragments of memories, but none of them seem real. It's as though I'm seeing clips from a movie about somebody else's life.'

Beth took his hand and squeezed it. 'Don't worry. You will remember everything soon, I'm sure.'

But then what will happen? she thought. *Will it be a case of returning to our old ways, of drifting even further apart? I love you, Dan, and I want you back. But I want the Dan I married — the fun loving, caring, passionate*

*husband; the doting father — not the
man who is continually absent.*

Dan lowered his head and gazed out
of the train window as they pulled up to
another platform. Beth felt him stiffen
beside her. 'Looks like we might have
company,' he said.

Beth's insides tightened as she saw a
man in an oversized parka, the hood
pulled up over his face, waiting in the
station and scanning the carriages as
they passed. With a hiss the doors slid
open, and two opposing rivers of people
fought against each other to get on and
off the subway train. Beth and Dan
watched as the man climbed into the
end carriage.

'Do you think it's him?' Beth said.

'I'm not sure,' Dan replied. 'I didn't
get a look at his face.'

'If it is the Ghost, I wonder if he saw
us.'

'I doubt it,' Dan replied. 'But I think
he may have an idea that we are on
here, and he'll be working his way up
through the carriages looking for us.'

'We should get off at the next station.'

'Yes, although he may well spot us getting off,' Dan said. 'If only I'd kept my suit on beneath this flaming Father Christmas outfit, I could have at least taken it off. I feel about as inconspicuous as a tarantula on a wedding cake in this thing.'

Hitching his red trousers up again, he took Beth's hand. 'Come on, let's head down to the front of the train. I don't think our friend the Ghost will take much time searching the carriages.'

They pushed their way through the packed carriage. There was lots of grumbling, and Beth was conscious of the stares that they got.

'Sorry,' she said. 'I'm ever so sorry.'

As they got to the end of the carriage, they pulled into another station. Dan opened the door between the two carriages, and Beth glanced back as shoppers got on and off the train.

'Dan, we haven't got time to get off the train,' she said.

'Let's just keep moving,' he replied. 'We'll get off at the next stop.'

The next carriage was just as full as the last one, but Dan didn't waste any time and plunged straight into the mass of bodies. They forced their way through, swaying with the motion of the train, the lights flickering occasionally. At one point they went out for what seemed like an age, although it could only have been a couple of seconds. Everyone groaned as they were plunged into darkness, and Beth's chest tightened as she remembered being chased through the catacombs, and the skeletons embedded into the walls.

At the end of the carriage, Dan struggled with the handle on the door. Feeling exhausted with the constant tension and running, Beth leant against the side of the carriage and closed her eyes. If only Dan's memory would come back, he could contact whoever it was that he worked for and get some help. Dan and Beth could be taken to safety, leaving his superiors to worry about the threat from the Order of Omicron, or whatever they were called.

'Got it!' Dan said as he opened the door and stepped through the gap between the carriages.

'Ooh!' Beth yelled as the panel she was leaning against suddenly gave way and she fell backwards. She tumbled into the arms of a fat man, who looked down at her and smiled.

'*Ce doit être mon jour de chance!*' he said. His breath smelt of booze, and he looked sleepy. Beth realised she had been leaning against a door to a toilet. She tried to pull herself away, but the man held onto her, seemingly intent on keeping her and taking her home as a prize.

'Let go of me!' she shouted, struggling to get out of his grip; but he was like an octopus, and wherever she turned there was another arm encircling her.

'*Je prends cela pour vous,*' he said, making a grab for the briefcase. '*Il doit être lourd.*'

Beth snatched the briefcase away from him before he had chance to take it. Where was Dan? Didn't he realise she wasn't behind him anymore? Beth panicked at the thought of losing him again, as she fought against the lecherous, drunken French man.

A red-suited arm shot through the doorway, the hand grabbing the man by his suit and hauling him out of the toilet.

'Merry Christmas,' Dan said, and planted his boot in the man's considerable backside, sending him tumbling into the commuters packed together like sardines in a tin.

'I thought I'd lost you again,' Beth said.

'Don't worry, I'm not leaving you behind,' Dan replied, taking her by the hand and leading her through the gap between carriages. 'How on earth would I deliver all those Christmas presents without your help tomorrow night?'

The two of them continued forcing their way through the crowded underground train until they had reached the final carriage, just as they were pulling into another brightly lit station.

'We'll get off here,' Dan said, peering through the window as the carriage slowed down.

Beth glanced over her shoulder, through the windows in the doors connecting the carriages. The Ghost was pushing his way through the crowded carriage, the hood of his parka still pulled up.

'He's in the next carriage,' Beth gasped as the train pulled to a stop.

'Don't worry, just stay close to me,' Dan replied. 'He probably hasn't seen us yet, and he will stay on the train and keep looking for us.'

She gripped Dan's hand anxiously as the doors slid open.

'You don't sound very convinced,' Beth said as they stepped out of the carriage and onto the platform.

'Sorry, I guess I'm going to have to work on improving my lying skills, right?'

'Don't you dare,' Beth replied. 'Having been fooled by you into believing you were the most boring husband in the world for the last few years, I'd say you're already too clever at hiding the truth from me.'

Dan pulled Beth into a shadowed recess and watched as the crowded platform gradually emptied of people. The train pulled out of the station, and as it slid past, Beth anxiously searched the windows for any sign of the Ghost pushing his way through the crowded carriage.

As people left the platform, more hurried onto it, waiting for the next metro train.

'I don't believe it!' Dan hissed. 'Look, he's here on the platform — he got off the train when we did.'

A cold shiver ran through Beth as she saw the man in the parka standing on the platform, his hooded head swivelling from side to side as he looked for them. Although she couldn't see his face, she could picture the waxy-looking skin, those dark eyes, and the pointed teeth glittering with diamond studs.

'It's like he absolutely knows we're

here somewhere, he just doesn't know where,' Dan whispered, pulling Beth deeper into the shadowed recess. 'Like he can smell us, or has a sixth sense.'

'I can hear another train coming — let's get on it. If we wait until the last moment, he might not see us.'

'Just like in my favourite movie, *The French Connection*, when Gene Hackman is following Fernando Rey on the New York subway.'

'Hey, you remembered something else!' Beth said as the train pulled into the station with a hiss of brakes and squealing of wheels on the tracks.

Dan looked down at Beth, and for a moment it was like the early days in their marriage, and she was sure she could see his eyes alight with love for her. Despite the fact that they were hiding in an alcove at a Paris train station platform from a hired assassin nicknamed the Ghost, and even despite the fact that Dan was dressed in a tatty Father Christmas outfit and smelt like an overripe pile of kitchen waste, Beth was suddenly overcome with an urge to kiss her husband. Did it matter that he couldn't remember who she was?

Beth stood on tiptoe and planted a quick kiss on his lips.

Dan's eyebrows scrunched up, a look that Beth was familiar with. It meant he was confused; that he needed a moment to try and process his thoughts. He didn't look at all pleased with the kiss.

'I'm sorry,' she whispered. Perhaps momentarily she had hoped that a kiss might kick-start his memory, but she was wrong.

'That's all right,' Dan replied. 'It was a perfectly nice kiss. I just wish I could remember, that's all.'

Any further conversation was halted as the alarm beeped to signal that the doors were about to close. Gripping Beth's hand tight, Dan pulled her out of their hiding place and leaped onto the train, between the doors sliding closed. Beth's heel got caught between the doors and they slid open again, prompting a groan from the passengers standing by them.

Beth held her breath, waiting for the doors to close once more and watching the Ghost, still standing on the platform with his back to them, searching the crowd for any sign of his quarry.

'We did it,' Beth said, jostled as more commuters and Christmas shoppers struggled to fit onto the packed carriage.

'Oh no, I don't believe it,' Dan groaned.

Beth followed his gaze, looking out of the window. There was another Father Christmas who had just got off the train and was heading for the exit. The Ghost was following him.

'He thinks he's you, doesn't he?' Beth said.

Dan nodded. 'And when he catches him, will he bother asking the poor man any questions, or will he just dispose of him — permanently?'

The alarm sounded, signalling the doors were about to close again.

Dan shoved his boot in the doorway, halting the sliding door. It automatically opened again, and Dan received angry looks and even more groans from the passengers.

'You stay here. I'll meet up with you at the end of the line.'

'No way,' Beth replied, pushing past him and jumping onto the platform. 'I'm not losing you again.'

Dan, still standing on the train, gazed at Beth in astonishment. The door alarm sounded again.

She waved at him urgently. 'Come on, quick!'

Dan jumped off the train just as the doors slid shut.

'Right,' Beth said, 'let's go rescue Santa!'

10

Beth was grateful to be back outside in the crisp, cold, fresh air. Down in the Underground it had been stiflingly warm, and she had felt suffocated and claustrophobic. Her hand ached from gripping the briefcase handle, and she was sure she was holding it too tight, painfully aware of the huge stash of euros inside.

They slipped through the crowds, past wooden market stalls decorated with fairy lights. The cold air was rich with the combined aromas of scented candles and mulled wine. One of the stalls was selling hot pork rolls, and Beth's stomach growled at the thought of biting down into one of them; already she could taste the stuffing and apple sauce.

They passed a group of carol singers standing in front of a large Christmas tree decorated with coloured lights, stars and angels. The men and women, wrapped up in heavy overcoats and scarves, white mist floating from their mouths, had beautiful voices. Even though she couldn't understand the words, Beth recognised the tune as 'Hark! The Herald Angels Sing'. All around them people laughed and smiled, children shouted with delight, and the snow drifted down in lazy, fat flakes of white; and Beth thought, *How wonderful! This is the best Christmas ever.*

'Hurry up, we're losing them!' Dan hissed, bringing Beth back down to earth with a jolt. He had hold of her free hand and pulled her along as he increased his speed. Back in the Underground, giving chase to rescue the other Father Christmas had seemed like a good idea. Beth knew that neither she nor Dan could have lived with themselves if they had left an innocent man to possibly die because of their inaction. But now that they were outside and in the middle of the chase, the obvious danger of what they were doing was giving her second thoughts. After all, they were now running after the very person who, just minutes ago, they had been running away from.

Suddenly they were free of the crowded market, and they burst onto a wide thoroughfare, a cobbled street with shops lining it, their windows glowing warmth and tempting cold shoppers inside. Beth could see the other Father Christmas up ahead, and cried out as she realised the Ghost had caught up with him. He was gripping him by the arms, keeping him moving at a fast pace. Suddenly they veered off left into a vast gothic church.

A Ghost and Father Christmas, going for prayers.

'Quick, before we lose them altogether!' Dan said.

They ran through the ornate doorway, past a sign informing them that they were entering the Saint-Denis Basilica, and into the nave. Heavy, solid stone pillars swept upwards to the arched ceiling. On either side of them were vast stained-glass windows, their colourful Biblical illustrations dulled by the overcast day. There was a choir practice in progress, the members of the group looking very casual in jeans and jumpers, the choirmaster readying them for another song.

Dan scanned the cathedral's interior, his sharp gaze quickly passing over the visitors milling up and down the aisles. The bright red of the Father Christmas should have been easy to spot, but he was nowhere to be seen.

Beth noticed the entrance to the crypt. There was a sign on a wooden plinth, in both French and English: 'Crypt Closed'.

'Do you think they might have gone down there?' Beth whispered.

'Let's find out,' Dan replied.

They hurried over to the stone staircase, their footsteps echoing through the vast cathedral space. At the top of the stairs, Dan paused and turned to Beth.

'It might be best if you wait here. I

have no idea what I am going to do when I get down there and confront the Ghost.'

'Won't your secret-agent fighting skills instinctively spring into action, just like back at the inn, when he first attacked us?'

'I have no idea,' Dan replied. 'But I think I am about to find out.'

He turned and ran down the steps, one hand clutching the waistband of his red trousers, holding them up, and the hems flapping around his ankles.

Beth sighed. There was no way she was staying up here, leaving Dan to fight a professional assassin whilst dressed as a rather tatty down-on-his luck Father Christmas.

She followed him down into the crypt.

Down beneath the church, the crypt was a maze of fat pillars and low vaulted ceilings. Beth was conscious of the mass of the cathedral above her and the weight of centuries that it had been standing. Dan was just ahead of her, darting between the smooth stone pillars. Their every movement echoed around the underground space, announcing their arrival. So much for stealth.

In the depths of the crypt, which in contrast to the catacombs was well lit, Beth could see two figures running away. Dan ran on ahead of her, still clutching his trousers. The men ahead of them stopped and turned. They had nowhere left to go.

The Ghost pulled his hood back, revealing his white wax-like features. He smiled, and his diamond-studded teeth glittered in the lights.

Beth scooted behind a pillar beside a table covered with a deep purple cloth and two large golden candlesticks sitting on top, and peered around.

The Ghost had a firm grip on Father Christmas's arm. Even beneath his big white beard, the poor man looked terrified. His hood had fallen off, and the white beard was askew on his face.

The Ghost watched Dan approaching him. His expression remained deadpan, perhaps frozen into place by all the plastic surgery he had had, but Beth thought she saw a momentary flicker of confusion in those dark eyes of his.

Then the realisation of his mistake dawned, and he let go of the frightened Father Christmas, pushing him contemptuously away. The poor man stumbled and fell on the hard floor. He wasted no time scrambling away from his captor. Facing Dan, the Ghost opened his mouth wide and snapped his pointed teeth together, making an unnerving clicking noise. And then, before Beth had even realised what was happening, he struck out with a fist. Dan dodged the blow and hit back, but his attacker had already moved out of the way.

The two men circled each other warily. They had both adopted fighting poses, like cats stalking each other, hackles up, ready to pounce.

Beth couldn't believe how fast Dan had moved or how easily he had slipped into fighting mode. Again she had the uneasy feeling that she had never really known her husband, and that he had been as much of a stranger to her before he lost his memory as he was now.

Both men were completely silent. Their feet whispered over the smooth stone floor of the crypt as they circled each other, keeping eye contact the whole time. The two men made a bizarre sight down in the burial chamber of a church, a waxen-faced man with diamond-studded teeth fighting Father Christmas.

The Ghost struck out again, this time with his foot, a karate kick aimed at Dan's hips. But Dan leapt out of the way and delivered a hand-chop to the other man's neck. The Ghost rolled to the floor and jumped to his feet again, a look of pure hatred on his face. His eyes burned with a dark intensity, and Beth knew he would kill them both if given the opportunity.

Dan dodged another swift attack, but

then stumbled. Before he could regain his balance his attacker was on top of him, hurling him to the floor.

Dan stood no chance now. Instinctively Beth grabbed one of the candlesticks and ran, screaming, over to the two men. The Ghost spun around as Beth swung the heavy candlestick at him. It slipped from her hand and the Ghost dodged out of the way. The gold candlestick smashed into the wall, just missing Dan's head and showering him with masonry dust.

'Whose side are you on?' Dan shouted.

'Oh no!' Beth gasped, stepping back, and into the Ghost's arms.

He pinned her arms by her sides, and his head was so close to hers she could feel his hot breath on her cheek. An image of those pointed, diamond-studded teeth appeared in her mind, and her knees went weak at the thought that he might bite her.

'It's me you want,' Dan said, staring intently at the assassin. 'Let her go, and take me with you.'

The Ghost said nothing. Beth wondered if he could speak; if maybe there was something wrong with his voice, or he had taken some bizarre vow of silence. His hands on her arms pinched painfully, and she had to clamp her teeth together to keep from crying out.

From the cathedral above them, the beautiful sound of the choir singing floated down to them as they started a new Christmas hymn.

'Let go of her, you creep!'

The Ghost rocked forward, his hands letting go of her arms, and collapsed on the floor. Dan grabbed Beth before she fell over, too.

Standing over the Ghost's prostrate body was the other Father Christmas, one of the big gold candlesticks in his hand.

'Hitting him over the head seemed like a good idea,' he said. 'Is he dead?'

'No, you knocked him out, that's all,' said Dan.

'Oh, that's a shame,' he continued in

his American accent, pulling off his beard. He was a small man, with a receding hairline and a ready smile. He stuck out his hand and shook with Dan and Beth.

'Are you all right?' Dan asked him.

'I am now.' He looked down at the body on the floor. 'Can you believe it? A mugger attacking Father Christmas! And what did he think he was going to steal from me? It's not like these suits have lots of pockets in them, right?'

'Uh, yes, right,' Dan replied.

'And have you seen his teeth? Do you think maybe he's one of those, what do you call them . . . Rap artists? Although calling them artists is doing the art world a huge injustice. I'll bet he's off his head on crack or something.'

'Are you sure he's alive?' Beth said, partly out of concern for the man, despite his intentions for her, and partly worried that he might suddenly leap to his feet and attack them again.

Dan bent down and took a good look at him. 'He'll be fine. He'll wake up with a sore head, that's all.'

'Good,' Father Christmas said. 'Maybe he'll think twice about attacking Father Christmas next time! By the way, my name's Al.'

'I'm Dan, and this is Beth.'

'Great,' Al said. 'Look, I know we should contact the police, but we're already late, and if we get involved in having to give witness statements and all that, we're going to miss the banquet. I say we get out of here quick, before he wakes up.'

'Banquet?' Beth said, puzzled.

'Didn't he tell you?' Al laughed. 'We always have a banquet on the second night of the convention. Haven't you got a suit with you? They won't let you in if you're not wearing your suit.'

Beth looked at Dan, and back to Al again, lost for words.

'Your Mrs Christmas outfit!' Al said, clearly growing exasperated. 'You are both here for the annual International Father Christmas convention, aren't you?'

'Yes, we are,' Dan said quickly. 'We were, um, looking for an outfit for Beth.

Someone stole hers earlier today.'

'It wasn't this guy, was it?'

'No,' Beth replied. 'It got stolen from our room at the hotel.'

'Really? Is nothing sacred anymore? So much for the season of peace and goodwill to all, huh? And hey, don't worry about the outfit; they'll have a spare one you can borrow at the convention centre.' Al glanced at Dan and wrinkled his nose. 'And while we're at it, we'd better see if we can find you a new one, too. Yours looks like it's seen better days.'

As they followed Al out of the crypt, Beth glanced at Dan, wondering what he was up to.

11

Beth had never seen so many Father Christmases in her life, never mind in one place before. But here they were, milling around, a sea of red and white and black. The convention centre was modern, all sleek glass and steel with a minimalist design — totally not what she would have expected for a Father Christmas convention.

But no one here seemed to mind. The convention was in full swing. Everyone had a glass of mulled wine, and there was lots of laughter and hugging and back-slapping, and shouts of 'Ho, Ho, Ho!' and 'Merry Christmas!'.

Beth noticed there was a significant representation by Mrs Christmas, too. She'd never heard of Mrs Christmas before, and supposed that she was an invention of the conference, a way of allowing the women to be involved in the dressing up. But where were the elves and Santa's little helpers?

As soon as they arrived, Al ran off in search of a Mrs Christmas outfit for Beth and a fresh Santa Claus outfit for Dan.

'What the heck are we doing here?' Beth whispered, when they were alone. She was still holding on to the briefcase full of money and, as much as she had kept swapping it from one hand to the other, her arms were aching.

'Think about it, Beth,' Dan replied. 'Dressed as Father Christmas, where better to hide out than at a Father Christmas convention?'

'Seriously? That's the best idea you've got right now?'

Even beneath his beard, which he had put back on as soon as they arrived at the conference centre, Dan looked hurt. 'Look, I know it sounds like a crazy idea, but we need to find somewhere to rest for a while and think about what we're going to do next.

We've been on the run pretty much since I woke up in hospital.'

'I suppose you're right,' Beth said grudgingly. 'But how long do you think we've got before someone notices they've got an extra Father and Mrs Christmas at the convention? I get the feeling these people take Christmas very seriously, and if we rile them we may end up wishing we were back fighting the Ghost again. And don't you think maybe we should have called the police? How do you think that freaky chap with the plastic face is going to feel when he wakes up with a sore head?'

'Quiet — Al's on his way back.'

Al arrived with two red outfits draped over his arms, and a huge grin just visible beneath his white beard. 'I knew I'd be able to find you some new out-fits. I can't believe you didn't manage to book a room here at the conference centre, but this our most popular year yet, so I suppose it's no surprise, really. Anyway, you can use my room to get changed in, but you'll need to be quick;

we're about to have pre-dinner drinks in the hall.'

A short, fat Mrs Christmas waddled up to them, beaming away. 'Oh, Al, is this the man who rescued you?' she gushed, throwing her arms around Dan and giving him a big hug.

'It sure is,' Al replied. 'He's a hero.'

'It was nothing,' Dan replied.

Hey, what about me? Beth thought, annoyed that no one was paying her any attention. *I was there too. I even threw a candlestick at that chap.*

Mrs Christmas released Dan from her hug and stepped back to take a better look at him. 'And you're so handsome, too!' she said. 'You look just like Roger Moore when he was James Bond.'

Beth groaned inwardly. If he raised an eyebrow at her, the woman might well faint with delight.

'Really?' Dan said, and raised an eyebrow quizzically.

Al's wife squealed, turned red and began giggling.

'Helen, we need to let Dan and Beth go and get changed or they'll be late for the drinks reception,' Al said, handing them their outfits and the key to his room.

'Now, do come and find us when you come down,' Helen said. 'I want to know all about you.'

'Of course we will,' Dan replied and raised his eyebrow, setting off another fit of giggles.

I don't believe it. You're actually starting to enjoy this, Beth thought, staring at Dan.

Once Beth had extricated Dan from Helen, they headed for the lifts.

'I am not wearing this stupid outfit!' Beth hissed. 'We need to get out of here as soon as possible.'

'Let's just get up to Al's room before we make any decisions,' Dan replied. 'At least we can freshen up there.'

They shared the lift in silence with a huge fat man in a reindeer onesie, complete with antlers on his head.

He turned and smiled at them.

Beth smiled back.

She wondered if maybe she was dreaming.

'Wow,' Beth gasped when they finally stepped inside Al and Helen's room. 'You could fit our entire house inside here.'

'It certainly is nice,' Dan said. 'Whatever Al does for a living when he's not dressing up as Father Christmas, it sure must pay well.'

There was a spacious lounge as well as a bedroom and a bathroom. Beth flopped down on the sofa and dropped the briefcase beside her. Now that she was sitting down she realised how exhausted she felt. Dan was right, they had been on the run for most of the day, and it was wonderful to be able to relax for a moment or two.

'I'm going to have a quick shower,' Dan said.

Seeming to forget for the moment that he was, in his amnesiac state, in front of a stranger, he stripped off the smelly Father Christmas outfit and dropped it on the floor. Beth gazed admiringly at his naked body as he crossed the room to the bathroom.

Now that she thought about it, she couldn't remember the last time she had seen him without his clothes on. They always seemed to go to bed at different times, and Dan had taken to wearing pyjamas or a T-shirt and shorts in bed. But looking at him now, she realised he had a fantastic, toned body.

Beth stifled a sudden urge to go and join him in the shower. Besides the thought that he would probably reject her because he couldn't remember their marriage, now wasn't really the time or place. And besides, if he welcomed her into the shower with him, despite still not remembering who she was, wouldn't that be tantamount to him having an affair?

Beth didn't like that feeling at all.

She stood up long enough to take off her coat and drop it on the floor, and then sank back down into the sofa again. She noticed a business card lying on the carpet next to her coat and leaned forward to pick it up. It was Parker's business card, which he had given her in the hospital. It must have fallen out of her coat pocket when she dropped it on the floor.

Beth turned the card over. On the back was Parker's mobile number, and underneath it another number with an international prefix. Was this the number for the organisation that Dan worked for? If she called it and explained the situation they were in, would they send help?

Beth turned the card over and over between her fingers. It didn't seem right that a secret government organisation would give away their telephone number on a business card. But what else could it be? Unless it was part of Parker's cover. But the number must connect somewhere, otherwise what was the point of it?

Dan was singing in the shower, something he used to do a lot of, but hadn't for many years. Although his singing was tuneless, Beth loved the sound of it. It reminded her of happier times.

Was this another sign that his memory was returning? They were both so stressed just running all the time, trying to work out who the good guys were and who were the bad guys, trying not to get killed by that freak the Ghost, it was no wonder that Dan couldn't remember anything. He just needed some time to relax — a good long sleep, maybe. Then his brain might be refreshed enough to allow the memories back.

Beth looked at the card again. They needed help. How long could they keep running for? And if Parker was telling the truth, and this cult was preparing a terrorist attack on the world leaders tomorrow night, they needed to find out how that was going to happen and prevent it.

Her mind suddenly made up, Beth picked up the telephone sitting on the mahogany table beside the sofa. The telephone was very old-fashioned, the black handset shaped like the silhouette of a gondola and resting in a cradle above the dial. But the numbers were push-buttons and bleeped like any modern phone when pressed.

Beth quickly dialled the number on the card, wanting to do this before Dan left the shower and talked her out of it. There was silence for a moment, and then a series of clicks and buzzes, before the ringing tone started.

After only three rings, the phone was answered. 'Hello, you have reached Cartwell International Shipping Agency.'

'Oh, hello,' Beth said, and then floundered.

The voice was recorded, an answer machine message. She listened despondently as it went through her options, wondering if this was a real company or cover for a spy department.

'For information on the cost of renting a shipping container, press one. If you are expecting a delivery and wish to know an arrival date, press two. For all other enquiries, and to speak to an operator, please hold the line.'

The voice was replaced by some in-offensive, bland pop music. Beth realised she was holding her breath as she waited, and let go, willing herself to breathe calmly and quiet her nerves.

'Hello, Cartwell International Shipping Agency. Can I help you?'

Beth stalled, her mouth open, not knowing what to say. This whole situation seemed so ridiculous, so utterly unbelievable. Was it possible that everything that had happened to her over the last couple of days had a perfectly reasonable explanation? Perhaps Parker really did work for a shipping agency, and was simply suffering some kind of delusional episode when he claimed to be a spy. Dan had lost his memory, and simply believed what Beth was telling him. But then what about the assassin called the Ghost, shooting the man in the café and chasing them across Paris?

And Tomato Peel? Was she suffering a delusional episode, too?

'Hello? Can I help you?'

'I . . . um, I . . . ' Beth stuttered.

'Have you got the number you need? This is Cartwell International Shipping. Is there anything I can help you with?'

The voice was female, and sounded efficient and calm. How was Beth going to explain to this woman that she was being chased around Paris by an assassin nicknamed the Ghost, who had a face like a mannequin's and diamonds in his sharpened teeth, with her husband who was dressed as Father Christmas, who had no memory of his life up until yesterday, but believed himself to be a secret agent?

'No, no, that's fine, thank you,' Beth said. 'Sorry about that, wrong number.'

And she hung up.

Dan stepped out of the bathroom wearing a towel tied around his waist, his hair wet and mussed up. Beth stuffed the business card in her pocket before he saw it. She felt like she had made a stupid mistake, but wasn't sure why, or what she had done wrong.

All thoughts of Cartwell International Shipping Agency disappeared as she gazed at Dan's muscular chest and his toned abdomen. He always had kept himself in shape, but he looked even fitter now, more muscular. Her insides ached with desire for him.

'You're certainly a lot less bashful than you were earlier,' she said.

'I suppose I am,' Dan replied, suddenly looking a little embarrassed. 'I think I will go and see if I can find anything to fit me out of Al's wardrobe.'

He disappeared into the bedroom, and Beth sighed.

Well, she thought to herself, *at least you're getting to spend some time with him. And it has been interesting, to say the least.*

But what was going to happen when his memory returned? What if their life went back to how it had been the last few years? Beth stuck at home, whilst Dan disappeared on secret trips abroad. The two of them settling into a mundane, middle-aged domesticity when he was back. Barely talking to each other, never going out together or having nights in, kissing and cuddling.

They might as well be divorced.

Dan walked out of the bedroom and spread his arms. 'Well, how do I look?'

Beth groaned and clapped a hand over her eyes. He was wearing a pair of beige slacks, a shirt with a black and white print on it that resolved itself into a randomly repeated picture of Marilyn Monroe, and a pair of slip-on shoes covered in palm trees.

'I think I preferred the smelly Father Christmas outfit!' she said, and started giggling.

Dan started laughing too, and soon they were both doubled up, howling with laughter.

'I know!' Dan gasped. 'But these were the best clothes I could find!'

'No!' Beth exclaimed, and started laughing even harder.

Dan staggered over to the sofa and collapsed on it next to Beth, and they both let the laughter take over, helpless in its power.

When she had finally calmed down,

Beth felt so weak she could hardly move, and had to wipe tears off her cheeks.

Her hand found Dan's, and they both turned and gazed into each other's eyes. Beth's tummy turned over. He was giving her 'that' look. The one he used to give her so often when they first started seeing each other, and in the early days of their marriage. The look that said, *I love and adore you. You are everything to me.*

Dan leaned forward impulsively and gave Beth a quick kiss on the lips. He followed that up with a longer kiss, until he broke away, his face suddenly clouded over with confusion.

'I wish I could remember,' he said sadly.

'You will,' Beth replied, trying to keep her voice light and gentle, despite the torment she felt inside.

Dan looked down at the clothes he was wearing. 'These really are awful, aren't they?' he said, clumsily changing the subject.

'They're pretty bad,' Beth replied.

'Well, at least when I put the new Santa outfit on, it will hide Marilyn and the trousers.'

'We're not really going downstairs and joining them for pre-dinner drinks, are we?'

'I think we ought to put in an appearance before we slip away,' Dan replied thoughtfully.

'But how are we going to escape? That Helen woman is going to be stuck to you like a magnet.'

'Maybe we could say the elves have called us — summoned us back because there's a gift-wrapping emergency at the North Pole.'

'I'm not sure you'll get away with that one,' Beth said. 'As loony-tunes as these people seem, I don't think they actually believe in Father Christmas.'

'Hmm, maybe you're right; perhaps we should just slip quietly away. Al is so grateful that I saved him from the Ghost, I think he wants to show me off to all his fellow Santas tonight.'

Beth stretched and resisted the urge to lie down. 'All I want is a nice hot bath and a luxurious bed to sink into. How likely do you think it is that there might be even just one flippin' hotel room left in Paris the night before Christmas Eve?'

'That reminds me, we haven't even had chance to have a look at how much money there is in that briefcase,' Dan said.

He leaned over and picked it up, and snapped the catches open. When he lifted the lid he let out a low whistle.

'I knew it was full of money, but I never realised there was this much.' He lifted a wad of notes held together with an elastic band out of the briefcase and rifled through it with his thumb. 'These are all €50 notes, and there must be at least thirty or forty in each pack.'

'How many packs do you think there are?' Beth said.

'A lot,' Dan replied. 'More than enough for us to book into the fanciest hotel in Paris, if we wanted to.'

'That seems like an awful lot of money to pay the Ghost to kill us.'

'But who's paying him? The Order of Omicron, or Tomato Peel? If our friend Parker is to be believed, they want to kill us anyway, as they think we know all about their plot to kill the majority of the western world's leaders tomorrow night.'

'Except we don't know, do we?'

'But they think we do, and that's what matters to them.'

'Can't we just go to the police and tell them everything we know?'

'I'm not sure,' Dan said thoughtfully. 'This whole thing sounds a lot bigger than the police.'

Beth sat back in the sofa, laying her head against the cushion. 'That's what Tomato Peel said, back at the hospital.'

'If only I could remember what my contact in the café told me.'

'I know.' Beth closed her eyes. 'This would be so much simpler if we could just restore your memory. Maybe you need another knock on the head. Do you want me to go down to the kitchens and borrow the heaviest frying pan they have? I could hit you over the head and see what happens.'

'Hmm, thanks for the offer, but I don't think so. Anyway, let's not worry about that too much. Right now we've got the lives of the western world's leaders to think about, and all the other people who will be in Notre Dame Cathedral with them. Their families, the security people, all the guests. You know, I think you're right — maybe we should go to the police. They may not believe us, they may not even be able to do anything, but we've got to try at least. We just can't sit on this information and do nothing with it.'

'We could call them now,' Beth said.

'No, I think I would rather try and explain this in person,' Dan replied. 'If we leave now, we can catch a taxi and ask to be taken to the main police HQ in the city. That way we might get somebody in authority to listen to us, rather than a jobsworth on the other end of the telephone.'

'All right. Let's do it now, shall we?'

Just at that moment there was knocking on the door. 'Hey, are you guys ready yet? We're all waiting for you downstairs.'

'Just a minute!' Dan shouted, leaping to his feet. 'Don't come in yet, we're not decent!'

'Decent?' Al exclaimed. 'What the heck have you two been up to in there?'

'Just had a shower, needed to freshen up, hope you don't mind!'

Dan started struggling into his new Father Christmas outfit, and mimed for Beth to do the same.

She shook her head. 'Why on earth do we need to put these on?' she whispered.

'I don't mind at all,' Al shouted from the other side of the door, and laughed. 'I didn't like to mention it, but I have to say you smelled a little ripe earlier on, that's for sure.'

'Because,' Dan hissed, 'I can't let Al see me wearing his clothes, and the only thing I have to cover them up with is the Father Christmas outfit he gave me, and it is going to look a little odd if you refuse to wear your Mrs Christmas outfit.'

Beth rolled her eyes and picked the red suit up, holding it gingerly, as though it might explode at any moment.

'Do I really have to?' she pleaded.

'Yes, you really have to,' Dan replied.

'All right,' she sighed as she began pulling on the red trousers. 'But this is so not what I intended for a romantic Christmas holiday in Paris.'

12

Rather than carry the briefcase with her anymore, Beth decided to leave it in the room for the moment.

'It would look very strange for me to be carrying it around at the drinks reception, anyway,' she said, just before they opened up the door for Al. 'We can come back for it later.'

Al exclaimed at how wonderful they both looked. He had obviously started in on the drinks already, as he was louder and heartier than before. He clapped them on the backs and guided them to the lift, talking a mile a minute about the magic of Christmas, and the spirit of the season, and how he couldn't believe that someone had tried to mug him — and in a cathedral of all places!

They shared the lift with the man in the reindeer onesie again. Beth wondered if there was a reindeer convention happening at the same time as the Father Christmas one, and if they would all get together tomorrow night and head out to deliver presents to the children of France.

The pre-dinner drinks were held in the Villard de Honnecourt suite. Beneath silver chandeliers glittering in the warm glow of candles and a roaring log fire, the vast room was filled with men and women dressed in Christmas outfits. There was a huge Christmas tree, decorated in red and gold and blue tinsel, and multi-coloured lights that faded tastefully in and out.

A glass of champagne was handed to Beth by a waiter as soon as she had stepped through the doors. She glanced at Dan, and she could see him automatically scanning the room whilst listening to Al yammer on. Even with no memory of who he was, his instincts were always to be aware of his surroundings, searching out possible threats.

A short, fat Mrs Christmas waddled over to them, with three more following her. Beth wondered what a grouping of Father Christmases would be called. A grotto of Santas? A bag of Father Christmases?

The short, fat Mrs Christmas turned out to be, of course, Helen. 'This is the man who saved my Al from being attacked by that awful mugger!' she exclaimed to her friends.

Dan pulled down his beard and smiled at them. 'Hello!' he said.

The three Mrs Christmases all cooed and giggled, as though they were in the presence of a movie star. Beth sighed. She might as well have been invisible.

'Isn't he handsome?' Helen squealed. 'And doesn't he look just like Roger Moore? Raise your eyebrow, for us, Dan, go on!'

'The name's Bond, James Bond,' Dan said in a deep, serious voice, and raised his eyebrow.

All three of the Mrs Christmases turned to each other with a squeal and giggled even more.

Beth gave Dan her hardest stare. This

was ridiculous. He was enjoying all this attention far too much.

'Hey, Dan,' Al said, 'it's no wonder you couldn't get a room here for the convention. Seems your registration has been mislaid.'

'Oh, really?' Dan replied.

'Yeah, which means no place setting for you or Beth at the dinner table, either. But don't worry, I sorted it all out. Now, you stick with me, I want to introduce you to some of the guys.'

'And you,' Helen said, taking Beth's arm, 'can come with us.'

'Oh, no, that's all right,' Beth said, glancing at Dan.

'Don't you worry, I'll look after him!' Al bellowed as he led Dan away.

'It's tradition,' Helen said, taking Beth in the opposite direction. 'Father and Mrs Christmas go their separate ways, before meeting again at the banquet.'

Beth looked back, but already she had lost Dan in a sea of Father Christmases.

The next half-hour passed painfully

slowly as the various women talked about the best way to cook the Christmas turkey (with a herby pork and apricot stuffing, apparently), the perfect recipe for mulled wine (an orange studded with cloves, six table-spoons of honey, a stick of cinnamon, and slices of orange and lemon with ground ginger), and were fake Christmas trees better than real ones (opinion was divided on this one).

Beth's mind drifted back home, and she wondered what Toby and Sophie were doing right now. She suddenly realised she missed them terribly, and that she didn't want to spend Christmas Day apart from her children. This would be the first Christmas ever that they had been apart.

She checked the time. Eight o'clock! How had it grown so late? They needed to get away from this mad gathering and alert the police to the potential threat at the Notre Dame Cathedral. Feeling hot and stuffy in her outfit, Beth cast her eyes around the room, looking for Dan.

Locating him was impossible though, as all the men were supposed to keep their hoods up and their beards on.

Beth's insides tightened as she suddenly spotted Tamara Peel and two men wearing dark suits and ties entering the suite. Tamara pointed to both sides of the room and sent the men off in separate directions, before heading into the mass of people.

They were obviously looking for Dan. But how on earth did they know he was here?

Beth's heart sank as she remembered the telephone call she had made to the shipping company. It had obviously been a cover after all, and the woman on the other end of the line, realising that something was up, had alerted her superiors. Then they must have traced the call to the hotel, and had come to investigate and see if Dan was here.

Pulling her red hood even further down to try and conceal her face, Beth made her excuses to Helen and began circulating through the crowd, heading for the end of the hall where the men were congregated. She had to find Dan, and then they could get out before they were found.

'Dan! Dan!' she called, pushing her way in between the men dressed in their red suits.

This was impossible. Looking for her husband here wasn't like searching for a needle in a haystack, it was like looking for a particular wisp of hay in a haystack.

Or, to be more precise, a particular Father Christmas in a hall full of Father Christmases.

There was nothing for it. It had to be done.

The beards had to come off.

Beth yanked at a white beard, surprising the man beneath it.

'Sorry!' Beth said, and turned and pulled the beard off his companion.

'What on earth are you playing at?'

'Trying to find my husband,' Beth said.

Two Santas, who had been standing with their backs to Beth, deep in discussion, turned around at all the commotion.

Beth took hold of both the big, bushy white beards covering their faces and lifted them up.

'I'm so sorry,' she said, 'but I need to find my husband.'

She pushed on through the crowd without waiting for a response from either of the two men. She had to move quickly. Who knew where Tamara Peel and her two men in black were?

But Beth was growing increasingly desperate. It was as though she was stuck in an interminable nightmare, a world populated with nothing but an endless line of Father Christmases. Beth wasn't sure she would ever be able to enjoy Christmas again.

In her frustration, she yanked hard at a beard.

But this one didn't come off.

'Ouch!' the man yelled.

'Oh no, I'm sorry!' Beth gasped.

The man glared at her from beneath his red hood.

'I do apologise,' Dan said, appearing beside Beth, slipping an arm around her shoulder. 'That is a very fine beard you have there.'

'It has taken me years to grow it to this length, and your wife almost pulled it out at the roots,' the man said.

'Sorry,' Beth mumbled as Dan led her away.

'What on earth's got into you?' he asked her. 'Someone came and found Al and told him there was a mad woman wandering around the hall emasculating all the men of their beards.'

'I was looking for you!' Beth hissed. 'We have to get out now. Tomato Peel is here with two men friends, and as none of them are dressed in red, I doubt they're here for the Father Christmas convention.'

'How on earth did she locate us?'

Beth quickly explained about the telephone call she had made. 'I was just trying to get us some help, but then I got flustered on the telephone, and I was too embarrassed to say anything to you.'

'All right, let's not worry about it,'

Dan replied as they headed out of the Villard de Honnecourt suite and left all the Father Christmases behind.

Beth had half-expected there to be more agents dressed in black waiting for them outside, but the lobby was empty. They walked quickly past the reception desk and out of the building. The cold air nipped at Beth's face, but the snow had stopped falling and the roads had been cleared.

'Look out for a taxi,' Dan said, his hand on Beth's back, keeping them moving. 'We'll get out of here and then pay the police a visit, tell them what we know.'

'Wait a minute,' Beth said, pulling up short. 'We left the money in Al and Helen's room.'

Dan stopped walking and seemed to deflate, his whole body slumping forward.

'I don't believe it,' he said. 'We just can't seem to get any breaks, can we? Everything's against us, at every step we take.'

'It's been fun, though, right?' Beth replied rather weakly.

'Fun?' Dan looked at her. 'Is this what married life is like with me all the time?'

'No, just the opposite.' Beth sighed and touched his face with her finger-tips. 'Most of the time you're not even around, and when you are it's like you're not really there. Today has been frantic, and confusing and sometimes downright scary; but yes, it's been fun. And even though you're absent because you can't remember a flipping thing about us, or anything else, you have been more here today, more present in my life, than you have in a long time. I love you, Daniel Ogilvy, whether you can remember who I am or not.'

Dan pulled the white beard he had still been wearing down, and tucked it under his chin. He smiled.

'That's a lovely thing to say, and I find it difficult to believe that I would be so neglectful of you normally.' He glanced back at the convention centre. 'But do you think we could continue this conversation some other time?'

'I'll go back in and get the briefcase,' Beth said.

'No, that's too risky. You wait out here and I'll get the money.'

'Don't be silly. Tomato Peel and her two friends are looking for Father Christmas, not Mrs Christmas. Give me the room key and I'll go.'

Dan regarded her for a moment or two, seemingly unsure. Then, his mind suddenly made up, he passed her the room key.

'I'll be waiting around the corner, out of sight. Be careful.'

'Yes sir,' Beth said, smiling.

She walked back inside, across the vast lobby, and straight for the lifts. For once, the man in the reindeer onesie was nowhere to be seen, and Beth arrived at Al's room without encountering a single soul. The key to the room was a white piece of plastic, like a credit card. She swiped it through the plastic box on the door and pushed it open.

Al and Helen's room was empty, just as they had left it. Beth wondered if they were sitting down to their banquet now, and if they had been missed yet. At the thought of the banquet, she suddenly realised she hadn't eaten all day and, as if in agreement, her stomach growled with displeasure.

This isn't the time to be thinking about food, Beth decided. She spotted the briefcase where she had left it, beside the sofa, and picked it up. Overcome with an intense suspicion that the briefcase had been emptied of all its money, she placed it back down again and snapped the locks undone, opening the lid. The wads of euros were still there, just as they had last seen them, and she relaxed a little.

Beth closed the briefcase and picked it up again. Now to get back downstairs and outside to Dan. She was going to be a little more conspicuous, dressed in her Christmas outfit and carrying a briefcase, but it couldn't be helped. If she took the outfit off, there was more chance that she would be spotted by Tamara. Beth decided it would be best just to keep hidden under the red hood.

She paused at the door before pulling it open. Although it had been exhausting, confusing, and at times terrifying, she hadn't been lying to Dan when she said that today had been fun, in a strange sort of way. And she had meant what she had just said to Dan. She did love him, still, after all.

But could it last? Once his memory returned and they went back to their old way of living, would that distance creep back and grow between them once again?

Beth gripped the door handle. Time to think about that later. First thing to do was get back to Dan, and then leave this place behind. Once they had told the police everything they knew about the plot to attack Notre Dame Cathedral while it was occupied by some of the world's most important leaders, they could relax and start thinking about the future.

Beth opened the door.

And came face to face with Parker, pointing a gun at her.

13

'Damn it, Beth! When are you going to stop running away from me and start trusting me?' Parker said, and put the gun away.

'Because you keep chasing us,' Beth replied, backing into the room.

'That's because I'm trying to help you.' Parker followed Beth inside. 'But Dan seems to think I'm the Devil incarnate, right? Look at yourself — he's got you chasing around Paris dressed in a Father Christmas outfit, carrying a briefcase full of cash.'

'Mrs Christmas.'

'Huh?'

'I'm Mrs Christmas, not Father Christmas.'

'Well, whatever. You could be dressed as Daffy Duck right now, but the point I'm trying to make is the same. You're being ridiculous. What I want you to do is take me to wherever Dan is hiding out right now, and then we can get you both somewhere safe and start working on recovering Dan's memory.'

'How do I know I can trust you?' Beth said.

Parker shrugged, and gave her a crooked smile. 'If I was the bad guy, wouldn't I have shot you by now and stolen all that money you're carrying around?'

'I suppose,' Beth replied thoughtfully.

'All right, now we're getting somewhere. Why don't you show me where Dan is, and then we can get the heck out of Dodge, before that Tamara woman finds us.'

'Aren't you on the same side?'

'No. She and her two goons are here to find you and Dan and wipe you both out. She's the double agent, Beth. Remember what I told you, back at the Café des Deux Moulins? The Order of Omicron want Dan killed before he upsets their plan. That's the only reason Tamara is here.'

'I thought she was here because I made that call to the number on your business card.'

'No, that alerted us to where you were, but I don't know how Tamara found you. She's no longer part of the organisation. Tamara has been found out, Beth, and right now she is more dangerous than ever. The important thing is, we need to get you both out of here, get you somewhere safe.'

Beth hated this situation. She had no idea who she could trust, but at the moment she had no other option but to go with Parker. He seemed to be telling the truth; but if he wasn't, what could she do?

'All right, I'll show you where Dan is.'

'Good girl.'

They took the lift down to the lobby. Beth half-expected to see Tamara waiting for them, but the reception was empty. Tamara and the two men with her must still be searching for them amongst the crowd of Father Christmases. Beth wondered if Tamara was yanking beards off faces, too.

When they got outside, and to the

spot where she had left Dan, he was nowhere to be seen.

'Where is he, Beth?' Parker said.

'I don't know,' Beth replied, the panic rising in her chest.

Had the Ghost found him and killed him? Or maybe he had been kidnapped, or mugged . . .

Dan stepped from the shadows, and in one swift movement he had removed Parker's gun from inside his jacket and pointed it at him.

'Hey, buddy, I see you're still dressed as Santa,' Parker said, holding his hands up.

'Have you got a car nearby?' Dan said.

'Listen, Dan, I'm just trying to help you out here.'

'By carrying a gun and chasing us halfway across Paris?'

'Bud if you'd just listen to me for five minutes, and let me explain — '

'Take us to your car. You're going to get us out of here.'

Parker shrugged. 'Okay. You're in charge.'

He led them to a large, sleek Toyota. The car bipped and the lights flashed as he opened it up.

'In the driving seat,' Dan said.

Parker did as he was told. Dan and Beth both sat in the back, Dan training his gun on Parker the whole time.

'Okay, drive,' Dan said.

Parker looked at Dan in the rear-view mirror. 'Where to, buddy?'

'Anywhere, just get us out of here. And stop calling me buddy.'

Parker sighed, and drove out of the convention centre car park.

★　★　★

They sat in silence in the car. Beth's stomach was a squirming knot of tension. She was seriously beginning to doubt that Dan knew what he was doing. Parker honestly seemed as though he was trying to help, but Dan wasn't able to trust him. In fact, so far the only person he had shown any trust in was Beth. That was lovely, but as she didn't actually know what she was doing, and had no knowledge of Dan's life as a secret agent, it was also worrying. Kind of like a case of the blind leading the blind.

Although the roads were clear, the rest of the city was blanketed in white. For the first time since she had arrived in Paris the clouds had cleared, and the night was bright, almost like daytime. The snow glistened beneath the full moon and the carpet of twinkling stars, and Beth thought how ironic it was that the setting was so romantic, but their situation was as far from it as she could think of getting.

She looked at Dan, who was staring intently at Parker. His brow was furrowed as though he was deep in thought, and it seemed the lines on his face had grown deeper over the last twenty-four hours. If it was stressful for her being in this situation, how much more traumatic must it be for Dan? After all, at least she could remember their marriage, their children. Dan could remember nothing and, on top of that, here they were trying to prevent a major terrorist attack, and he had no idea who he could trust.

Except for the police. Surely they could trust the police?

'Dan?' Beth whispered.

Her husband turned and looked at her, his face still scrunched up in thought.

'Why don't we get Parker to take us to the police station? At least we can report what we know, and they can take steps to protect everyone at Notre Dame tomorrow evening.'

'The police?' Parker said, glancing in the rear-view mirror at them. 'There's absolutely no point in me taking you to the police station.'

'Why's that?' Dan said.

'Because the peace summit has been cancelled. Someone higher up took the threat to the world's leaders seriously enough, even though it is still massively unsubstantiated. The carol service at Notre Dame is off; the peace summit is being rearranged; the President, the Prime Minister, they're all on their way back home for Christmas, even as we speak. It's over Dan. It's all finished.'

'How do I know that? Why should we trust you?'

'Let me turn the radio on, find a news channel. It's all over the news right now.'

Parker switched the radio on and scanned through the frequencies until he found what he wanted. The male voice was speaking in rapid French, and Beth couldn't understand a word of it. But as Dan listened intently to what was being reported, the set of his face began softening.

He turned to Beth. 'He's telling the truth. The peace summit has been cancelled due to intelligence reports of a suspected terrorist attack.'

'Oh, thank goodness for that,' Beth said, breathing a sigh of relief.

'Now do you believe me?' Parker said.

Dan was still pointing Parker's gun at

him. He lowered it, but only a little.

'I suppose so,' he said.

Parker pointed to a collection of lights on the road ahead of them. 'Why don't we stop off at the service station? We can grab a coffee, a bite to eat, and we can talk some more about this. And for crying out loud, buddy, will you stop pointing that gun at me? You're making me nervous.'

★   ★   ★

Over coffee and croissants, Parker explained everything.

'We'd been hunting down the double agent in our midst for months. It was ironic, really; we had one of our guys posing as a member of the Order, and they had one of their guys posing as an agent in ours.'

'Surely you did security checks?' Dan asked.

'Of course. We did just that — an intensive background security check on everyone in the service, from the janitor on up to Mission Control, as we like to call the head bods. Nothing. Everyone was clean.'

'But your man discovered the identity of the double agent in Section 13, didn't he?'

'That's right. And in another stroke of irony, their guy discovered the identity of our man working undercover in the Order at about the same time. That meeting you had with our contact in the Order was supposed to fill in the blanks. Sean was going to tell us everything he knew about the terrorist plot, and the name of our mole.'

'Sean? That was his name?' Beth said.

'Yeah, Sean Miller. He was ex-SBS, as tough as they come.'

'SBS?' Beth asked.

'Special Boat Service, similar to the SAS, but tougher. Sean had been living as a member of the Order for a couple of years. He'd severed all ties with his family and friends and colleagues, and he was in so deep we had no way of contacting him or even knowing if he

217

was still alive. But then one day last week we got a message in London from him saying he needed an urgent meet, and that we should get him out. Dan, Sean was meant to come back with you and you were going to accompany him home, back to England, on the next flight.'

'Oh no,' Beth said. 'And then I turned up and spoilt everything.'

'You were a surprise, granted,' Parker replied. 'But you didn't spoil anything. None of us could have stopped that hit man taking Sean out. We were just lucky he didn't kill you, too, Dan.'

'It was horrible,' Beth said, the memory of that night still sharp in her mind. 'Seeing Sean being killed, expecting Dan to be shot next. It was like watching an action movie in slow motion; everything felt so unreal when I saw him pulling that gun out and pointing it in the café. And then when he turned and ran straight into me and we fell over, I thought he was going to kill me next.'

'I know. It must have been a traumatic

experience for you.'

'It was awful — but nothing compared to being hunted by him on the metro earlier. He's so scary-looking, with those diamond studs in his teeth, and his face so stiff and shiny.'

'Don't worry, we've got people hunting him down. We'll catch him, I'm sure.'

Dan yawned. 'This is a lot to take in, and I feel exhausted.'

'Me too,' Beth said. 'We've been on the run all day; and with the stress, too, it's no wonder we're tired.' She pulled her mobile out and activated the screen. There was a new text message waiting for her from Sara.

'What I don't understand,' Dan said, 'is why you can't just arrest any members of the Order that you find. If they are paying someone like the Ghost to find and kill people, and plotting terrorist attacks, they need clamping down on, right?'

'Because they are ostensibly a peaceful organisation. They don't have

219

religious status, but they are an official charity. According to the leaders of the Order, those guys running around causing mayhem and violence and threatening terrorist attacks are an extreme wing of the cult. If we went around and arrested every member of the Order that we found, we'd wind up in big trouble and probably be taken to the European Court of Human Rights for harassment, discrimination, you name it. That kind of legal snafu we don't need.'

Beth stood up. 'I'm just going to phone home and check on the children. I'll be back in a minute.'

As she walked away she heard Parker saying, 'Me and you, Dan, we go back a long way. I'll sure be glad when you've got your memory back, and we can have a drink and share some of the old stories again.'

Beth dialled her home number and Sara picked up.

'Hi, Beth!'

'Hi, Sara. Just phoning in to check on

you guys and say hello.'

'Oh, don't worry about us, we're all great here. I didn't expect a call so soon from you again. Is everything okay?'

Beth struggled to remember the last time she had called. Had it been yesterday, or the day before? With a sudden shock, she realised it had only been earlier today, at the café with Parker. So much had happened in such a short space of time. She yawned again, a wave of tiredness washing over her.

'Beth? Is everything all right?'

'Hmm? Oh yes, everything's fine. I forgot I called earlier, that's all. It's been such a busy day.'

'It must be so exciting out there. I bet you're having a wonderful time. And Paris, is it as beautiful as they say it is?'

'It's lovely,' Beth replied, stifling another yawn.

'Tell me, what are you looking at right now? Describe what you can see for me, so I can feel like I'm right there with you.'

Beth gazed at the empty tables

stretching out across the café. The place looked tired and old, and like it was shutting down for the night. Parker was still talking intently to Dan, who was taking a sip of his coffee.

'It's beautiful,' Beth lied, not wanting to explain where she was, or why. 'I'm in our hotel room and I can see out of the window, and it's snowing, and — '

'Oh, wait, Toby wants a quick word.'

Beth was grateful for the interruption.

'Hi, Mum!'

'Hi, Tobes,' Beth said, and clutched her mobile tighter as she struggled to keep her voice even and light. The sound of her son's voice reminded her how much she missed them and wanted to be with them, especially tomorrow, on Christmas Eve. 'What are you guys up to?'

Beth only half-listened as Toby rattled on about his day, and about how he couldn't wait for Christmas morning so that he could open his presents. She watched Dan and Parker talking, although it seemed to be Parker who was doing all the talking. Dan looked utterly exhausted, as though he might fall asleep at any moment, and Beth was feeling the same way.

'That's nice,' she said when Toby had finished talking, but not having any idea what he had just told her.

'Beth, are you sure you're okay?' Sara said when she got back on the phone.

'Oh, yes, I'm fine,' Beth said, and sat down on the nearest chair as her vision began to sway and blur and a tidal wave of sleepiness overcame her. 'Everything is wonderful. I've got to go now, but I'll call again tomorrow.'

Beth hung up and pocketed her mobile. The excitement of the last couple of days was really catching up with her now, and she felt like she could fall asleep where she was. Looking up, she saw Parker approaching her. But now there were two of him, floating together and then apart, and he was reaching out a hand to her and saying something.

After that, Beth remembered nothing more.

14

Beth's eyes were glued shut, and her body was a lead weight. She tried shifting position in the bed, but gave up when she realised it would take too much effort to roll over. She had been sweating as though she'd had a fever, or maybe the heating had been left on all night and the bedroom had become stuffy and hot.

A marching band had been tramping through her head all night, too, banging drums and playing on the trumpet, and generally making enough noise to give her a blinding headache.

Was this a hangover? Beth couldn't remember being at a party last night, but she had to have been. There was no way she would drink so much alcohol normally, to be suffering this much when she woke up.

Summoning every little scrap of

energy she could find, Beth rolled over, and her arm found her husband lying beside her. She draped her hand over his chest. This was nice. So often these days Dan came to bed late and left early in the morning, before they had a chance to talk or just snuggle up in bed with each other. And then he was away so often, too.

It would be nice if he was staying at home today. Perhaps they could do something together, for once. Spend some time rebuilding their relationship, discovering each other once more. If only he didn't have that stupid Paris trip coming up. Going away at Christmas, of all times.

A tiny worm of unease squirmed into life at the back of Beth's mind.

Paris.

What was wrong with that thought? Why did it turn her stomach over — or was that just the hangover?

Dan mumbled and shifted position slightly.

Paris. At Christmas.

Suddenly the memories of the last couple of days flooded back, her mind snapping to attention, and Beth opened her eyes, squinting against the grey light. She struggled up into a sitting position, the bedclothes falling from her.

They were in a cheap hotel room. Thin curtains had been drawn across the window, doing nothing to prevent daylight spreading through the room. Beth looked at Dan. Like her, he was still wearing the Christmas outfit. No wonder she had been sweating, lying under a duvet with two layers of clothing on.

What was going on? Where was Parker?

'Dan!' Beth hissed, gripping his shoulder and shaking him.

Dan mumbled something and tried to shake her off.

'Dan, wake up!' Beth said, louder this time.

He slowly opened his eyes and turned his head to look at her. 'Beth?'

His voice was thick, and slurred, like he had been drinking too much, too. 'What time is it? Am I late for work?'

'Um, no, not really,' Beth replied. 'In a way, you're sort of already at work.'

The confusion in Dan's eyes began clearing and he said, 'Oh no, we're in France, aren't we?' He covered his face with his hands. 'It's all coming back, I can remember everything!'

'Everything?'

'Yes — I remember you turning up at the hotel, and the argument. Then you followed me, didn't you? And you were in the car when we crashed.' He looked up at her. 'Are you all right? Were you hurt?'

Beth shook her head. She couldn't speak. She didn't know whether to cheer or cry, knowing that his memory had returned.

Dan pulled the duvet back and sat up, swinging his legs over the edge of the bed, his back to her.

'Parker! Is he here still?'

'I don't know. I don't think so.'

Dan twisted around to look at Beth. 'He's the double agent. He's the traitor.'

'How do you know?'

'Because I can remember it all now! Sean told me everything in the café. Parker had been recruited only recently by the Order, and he's been feeding them information. That was why Sean made contact and wanted to be pulled out so urgently. The Order knew he had been spying on them, and they were hunting him down.'

'And then they killed him,' Beth said. 'Oh, that poor man.'

Dan clenched his fists and stood up. He looked murderously angry. 'I'm going to catch him. Sean was a good man; he had a family. I'm going to catch Parker, and he will pay for this.'

Beth had never seen Dan looking this way before. It frightened her a little, that he appeared to have so much barely controlled rage inside of him, and it scared her even more at the thought of it being released.

'But I don't understand,' she said. 'If Parker is a traitor, one of the bad guys, why did he keep after us, chasing us around Paris? And why did he want to help us?'

'I don't know,' Dan muttered.

'Surely he could have killed us any time he wanted, but he didn't.'

Dan didn't say anything. Instead he began pacing up and down the tiny room.

'And why did he leave us here?' Beth got out of the bed and walked over to the window. She parted the curtains. 'Wherever here is.'

Dan stopped pacing. 'Beth, the money in the briefcase. Have you got it still?'

Beth's eyes widened as she looked around the small room. 'No, it's gone.'

'Damn it!' Dan muttered, and started peeling off his Father Christmas outfit.

Beth watched him with a growing sense of despair. Now that his memory had returned, he seemed to have reverted to his old, distant self. Or was she expecting too much of him? After all, he had just awoken in a strange room, his memory

229

only now returning. She had to give him time, not push him.

He looked at her. 'What are you waiting for? Get out of that suit, and then we can get out of here.'

'Where are we going?'

'We need to get back to Paris; put a stop to Parker's plan.'

'His plan?' Beth gazed at Dan, confused. 'But his plan's finished, he told us himself. The peace summit has been cancelled because of the security threat.'

'No, that was a lie to throw everyone off,' Dan replied, looking grimmer than she had ever seen him. 'The real plan happens later tonight, in the centre of Paris.'

'But what is it?'

'The Order of Omicron are planning to topple the Eiffel Tower during a Midnight Mass around its base. Not only will France's most famous landmark be destroyed, but thousands of people are going to die.'

15

It turned out they were at the service station where Parker had stopped off and bought them a coffee. The café was deserted, the lights low, with just a couple of staff in attendance. Through the large windows, the surrounding landscape looked like a winter wonderland. The rolling hills were white, and the trees were covered in heavy layers of snow. Even the motorway was covered in a thick layer of snow. Looking at the grey sky overhead, Beth suspected there was more snow on its way.

Dan had a brief conversation in rapid-fire French with one of the staff at the serving counter. When he returned he was frowning, and Beth's heart sank even further. Whatever he had found out, it wasn't good news.

'It seems we not only slept through the night, but most of the day, too. It's four thirty in the afternoon. Parker must have drugged us, put something in the coffees he bought us.'

'Dan, it's Christmas Eve — the Mass is tonight.'

'I know.' He stared at her. 'Have you got your mobile on you?'

Even as she searched for it, she already knew the answer. 'No, Parker must have taken it.'

'We need to get in touch with HQ and warn them of the danger.'

'There must be somebody around here with a phone.'

Dan turned back to speak to the staff at the serving counter, but metal shutters had been pulled down, and the lights behind it turned out.

They glanced around the deserted station. Outside, the light was growing dim. The service station looked like it had been closed down for the Christmas holidays. Beth had thought these places never closed, but maybe this one did.

'Come on,' Dan said. 'Let's have a good look around. There has to be a telephone somewhere.'

They walked through the deserted shopping area, the softly glowing lights over the display stands the only sign that there had once been life there. Dan found a telephone attached to a wall, but when he lifted the receiver he got nothing but silence.

'Maybe the telephone lines are down in the heavy snowfall,' Beth said. She looked out of the window, at the car park covered in snow. There was a single car outside, a thick layer of snow on its roof and over its windows.

'There must be somebody here. Look at that car,' she said.

Dan opened the door, a cold breeze ruffling their hair. 'Let's go and have a look,' he said. 'Maybe we can use the car to get out of here.'

'What do you mean? Steal it?'

Dan said nothing. He tramped through the deep snow, his breath streaming in white clouds around his head before being whipped away by the wind. Beth followed him. The only sound was that of their feet crunching through the snow. It seemed like the whole world had come to a standstill; like they were the only ones left alive.

She shivered. When they left the hotel they had been wearing their Christmas outfits, and had not brought their winter coats with them. Now that they had taken the red and white outfits off, they had no protection against the cold.

As they reached the car, Beth felt the first cold flakes of fresh snow caressing her cheek. She looked up and saw more snowflakes falling gently down.

Dan used his sleeve to wipe a clear space in the windscreen, and then shouted and jumped back.

The Ghost was sitting in the driver's seat, his hands on the steering wheel, staring at them and grinning, the diamond studs in his pointed teeth glittering.

'Run!' Dan shouted. He grabbed Beth's hand and pulled at her, dragging her through the snow, away from the car. Beth heard the car door opening behind them, and then beside them there was a soft explosion of snow on the ground.

He was shooting at them!

They reached the edge of the car park, where the ground sloped away towards a forest, the trees heavy with snow in their branches. As soon as they started running down the hill, Beth lost her footing, slipping in the snow. She fell over, taking Dan with her, and they both rolled and skidded down the steep slope. Freezing clumps of snow battered her face and her neck, and streamed down her collar.

They landed, breathless, at the bottom. Dan immediately jumped to his feet and hauled Beth up. Another small explosion of snow to their left, and she knew that the Ghost was standing at the top of the hill, shooting at them.

'Into the trees!' Dan gasped, hauling Beth along after him.

Her lungs burned with sucking in freezing cold air, and her heart hammered in her chest. They stumbled through the snow, Beth's back tingling from the trails of wet snow against her skin, and the thought that at any moment a bullet might slam into her, throwing her to the ground and stopping her heart forever.

They made it under the cover of the trees, slivers of bark exploding from a tree trunk in front of them as another bullet narrowly missed them.

Dan dragged Beth deeper into the forest, dead branches and twigs cracking beneath their feet as they stumbled between the densely packed trees. In here, beneath the canopy of branches laden down with snow, gloom descended upon them. Dan had to slow down due to the lack of visibility, but still dragged Beth after him at a dangerous speed. She was certain they would crash head first into a tree trunk at any moment and knock themselves out.

But despite the darkness and the uneven ground, Dan seemed to be able to navigate his way through the forest without colliding into a tree. He twisted this way and that, pulling Beth in close, whispering urgent commands to keep going, keep running.

After another minute of mad scrambling through the undergrowth, Beth sank to her knees in exhaustion. 'I can't go any further!' she gasped as her hand slipped out of Dan's. 'Please, let me rest for a minute or two.'

Dan squatted down beside her. She could just see him in the darkness, a grey shadow amongst the twisted dark shapes of the branches, like monstrous claws frozen in time.

'We have to keep moving,' he hissed. 'If we don't keep running he will kill us!'

Beth sucked in freezing air, filling her lungs. 'I just need a minute, please,' she said, the words coming out in a tortured wheeze.

'Okay, okay, just one minute.' He took her hand and motioned for her to be as quiet as possible, then listened intently. Beth was surprised he could hear anything over the jack-hammering of her heart.

'I don't think he followed us,' Dan whispered.

Beth's heartbeat was beginning to

slow down and her breathing get calmer. 'Good,' she whispered back. 'What do we do now?'

'We need to find a road, one that's cleared of snow, and see if we can hitch a ride back to Paris, or at least get the driver to make a call for us. We're running out of time.'

Beth struggled to her feet. The dash through the forest had caused her to break out into a sweat, and now she felt chilled. For the first time she wished she had kept her Mrs Christmas outfit. She looked at Dan, still wearing the clothes he had 'borrowed' from Al back at the convention. Neither of them was wearing an overcoat, and it was freezing cold.

'We need to get inside somewhere warm,' Beth said.

'Come here,' Dan replied, and wrapped his arms around her. 'I'll do my best to keep you warm.'

They struggled through the forest, their feet crunching through the frozen undergrowth. Occasionally they brushed against a branch covered in snow, and a gentle shower of white snowflakes covered them. Walking on in silence, Beth felt secure and protected in Dan's embrace.

Other than the sounds they made, the forest was silent. The deeper into it they walked, the more Beth began to worry that they would never find their way out. And, despite Dan's best efforts, she was growing increasingly cold. Her teeth began to chatter, and she started shaking uncontrollably. Dan tried rubbing her arms and wrapping more of himself around her, but that just hampered their progress.

'Keep going, Beth, please,' Dan said after a particularly violent shivering fit.

'D-d-do you e-even know where w-w-e are g-g-going?' Beth said.

'No,' Dan admitted. 'But if we stop moving, there's every chance the Ghost will catch us, and then we're dead.'

They struggled on, and it seemed to Beth that they were caught in an endless nightmare; that they would spend the rest of eternity stumbling through this dark, freezing forest.

'Look, can you see that?' Dan whispered.

Beth strained to see, only aware of the dark shadows of the trees surrounding them. But then, after a few moments she became aware of a faint, flickering orange glow between the tree trunks.

'Is it a f-f-fire?' Beth said.

'I don't know,' Dan muttered thoughtfully. 'Let's find out.'

They pushed on through the forest, the orange glow slowly growing stronger. Then they were free of the trees, snow falling gently down on them. The afternoon light had grown even gloomier whilst they had been under the canopy of snow-covered branches, but there was still enough light to see the fields blanketed in white stretching ahead of them. Up ahead, through the curtain of snowflakes, they could see what was making the orange glow.

'It's a hot air balloon!' Beth said.

The huge, colourful balloon was still tethered to the ground whilst a man and a woman bustled around it, making last-minute adjustments. A small dog ran around their feet, yapping excitedly. Occasionally the gas element flared even brighter, and they could hear the roar of the flame as it filled the balloon with hot air.

'It's beautiful,' Beth said.

There was a loud crack as a branch in the forest behind them, snapped. Beth heard a tiny zing, like a bee flying past her ear at supersonic speed, and there was a puff of snow in the ground just ahead.

'He's found us!' Dan hissed, grabbing Beth and hauling her closer to him.

Beth expected him to run for the hot air balloon, dragging her with him, but he didn't. Instead he ran to their left, crashing through the undergrowth between the trees, and pushed Beth down low, crouching down beside her.

Apart from the distant roar of the gas burner, its flame heating up the huge balloon, there was silence. Beth clutched Dan's hand, trying hard to control the shivering, and clenching her jaws to stop her teeth chattering. Dan put his finger to his lips and let go of her hand. Slowly and carefully he took a good grip with both hands on a slender branch sticking out over the path they had just come through and pulled it back.

After what seemed like an absolute age of waiting, Beth opened her mouth, about to ask what they were waiting for, when she saw the Ghost appear silently from between the trees, little more than an arm's length away. He was staring intently ahead, looking at the couple and their hot air balloon, and he was holding a large black handgun, cradling it against his chest.

Dan let go of the branch and it sprang forward, whipping the Ghost across the face in a flurry of snow. He fell to the ground, dropping the gun. Dan lunged for it, but the Ghost kicked out at Dan's ankles, and he stumbled and fell over.

Both men scrambled to their feet, hampered by the closely packed trees and the uneven ground. Dan glanced at the gun, lying in the snow. It was just out of reach for both of them. As Beth watched, terrified, she saw the Ghost grinning at Dan, and she realised she had never once heard him speak.

Suddenly the Ghost put his head down and dived at Dan, ramming him in the stomach. He crashed into a tree, a cloud of powdery snow and ice showering both men. Dan was on the defensive now, and the Ghost quickly overcame him, grabbing his arms and pinning them over his head against the tree trunk. Beth watched, horrified, as the Ghost opened his mouth wide, showing Dan his pointed teeth.

Was he going to bite him?

She made a mad scramble for the gun. The Ghost's head whipped around as he heard her and he let go of Dan, lunging for Beth.

Dan jumped on top of him and they rolled over in a flurry of snow. Beth gingerly picked up the black handgun. She had never held one before and immediately hated its cold, hard touch, and the smell of oil. She placed her finger against the trigger, and the gun jerked out of her hands as it fired. The bullet slammed into a tree close by, and Beth cried out in shock.

The two men looked up in surprise at the sound of the gun firing. Dan recovered first and grabbed the Ghost in an arm lock, twisting him face down into the snow and bending both his arms up painfully behind his back. He sat on the Ghost's back for a few moments, breathing hard.

'What are we going to do with him?' Beth whispered.

'Leave him here,' Dan replied. 'We don't have time to deal with him. We have to get to Paris as quickly as possible. Pass me the gun.'

Beth gingerly picked up the gun from where it had fallen in the snow, taking care not to touch the trigger. She passed it to Dan. As he reached out to take it from her, the Ghost bucked and heaved, throwing Dan off his back.

Beth screamed and dropped the gun, and it disappeared into a snowdrift.

'Run!' Dan shouted, struggling to control the assassin as he fought.

Beth turned and made a dash for the old couple and their hot air balloon. The woman had picked up the dog and was putting him in the basket. Then she climbed in as well.

'Hey, wait!' Beth shouted, her lungs aching with the effort of running.

The man turned around, his mouth an open 'O' of surprise.

Beth glanced back. Dan had managed to escape from the Ghost and was sprinting across the snowy field towards them. The Ghost was just behind, closing the distance between them at an alarming rate.

Beth started running again, but her legs felt like frozen lumps of meat, and she stumbled and almost fell. Her lungs were burning from the icy cold air she was sucking in with each strangled breath.

'*Was ist los?*' the old man said as Beth reached him. He was wrapped up in a thick winter overcoat and had a scarf wound around his neck, and a fur hat with flaps covering his ears.

Freezing cold and shivering violently, Beth had never felt so envious of anyone in her whole life. 'You've got to help us!' she gasped, clouds of white steam billowing around her face as she spoke. 'That man back there is trying to kill us.'

The woman, similarly attired to her husband, peered through the falling snow. 'She is right, Franz!' she shouted, pointing a gloved finger into the fading daylight. 'There is a man chasing them!'

'Into the basket, quick,' Franz said.

The man and woman both spoke in clipped German accents. Franz helped Beth climb up and over the lip of the wicker basket. The heat on her face from the propane burner was a welcome relief from the cold.

'Oh, you poor dear, you must be freezing,' the woman said. Seemingly heedless of the immediate danger of a man pursuing them, she pulled a blanket out of a hamper and wrapped it around Beth's shoulders, fussing over her like a mother hen. The dog, a black and white terrier, ran around Beth's feet, barking.

'In! In!' Franz commanded Dan, as he reached the basket, almost paralysed with exhaustion and cold.

Dan clung on to the sides of the large wicker basket and glanced back. The Ghost was almost upon them, grinning at them as he ran.

'No, you first,' Dan said, and helped Franz climb into the basket.

Then he turned back to face his pursuer, knowing he didn't have time to get inside the basket before the Ghost reached him.

Dan had a split second to see his pursuer charging at him before he was slammed against the wicker basket's side, rocking it slightly as it pulled against the ropes tethering it to the ground.

Beth screamed, and the dog barked.

Dan kicked out, his boot connecting with the Ghost's face, snapping it back.

Franz turned up the heat on the propane burner and the balloon lifted slightly, straining against the ropes.

'Dan, look out!' Beth shouted.

Dan blocked a hand chop from the Ghost but didn't see the kick coming, and the Ghost's booted foot smashed into his kneecap. A bolt of pain shot through the joint, and Dan's leg crumpled beneath him; he fell face down in the snow. On instinct he rolled over — just in time, as the Ghost's boot smashed into the place where Dan's head had been just a moment before.

Dan grabbed the assassin's ankle and yanked, pulling him over so that he fell hard on his back. The Ghost made a whooshing noise as the breath exploded from his lungs.

'Dan, get in the basket!' Beth screamed.

Dan looked up at the sound of her voice, but before he had chance to move he was overpowered by the Ghost. The latter's smile had gone and he snarled at Dan, the diamonds in his teeth glinting in the light from the flame.

Franz began untethering the basket from the stakes holding it to earth.

Dan and the Ghost were rolling around in the snow, throwing punches at each other. Beth could hardly see them through the eddies of swirling snowflakes and all the snow they were kicking up as they fought. She hugged the blanket around herself whilst Franz's wife continued to fuss around her as though having two men rolling around on the ground and fighting beside her was an everyday experience.

'Please don't leave him behind,' she begged Franz as she saw him untying the ropes.

'Do not worry, young miss,' he said. 'I am simply getting us ready to rise into the air as soon as your friend is free of that man.'

Dan did not look as though he was going to be free anytime soon, though. The Ghost stood up, hauling Dan to his feet by the scruff of his neck. He twisted him around, encircling Dan's neck with his arm, and began squeezing. Dan fought weakly, only succeeding in pushing the Ghost's back against the side of the basket. Beth could see he was too exhausted to keep fighting. The stress of the last few days, of being continually on the run, had taken its toll on him.

The German woman looked at the two fighting men and tutted. Then she picked up a spare propane canister and whacked the Ghost over the head with it. There was a dull, flat thud as it connected with his skull, and he keeled over, falling face first in the snow.

Dan leapt for the basket, crying out at a sudden shooting pain in his knee, as Franz released the final knot and the ropes unravelled. The balloon began to lift, rising from the earth as if by magic. Dan was just hanging on, his forearms over the edge of the basket.

Franz grabbed Dan by the forearms and began dragging him inside. Dan was halfway in when the basket suddenly lurched to one side, and he was dragged backwards by an unseen force. Beth screamed and rushed forward, grabbing Dan's arms along with Franz. Over the lip of the basket she could see the Ghost hanging on to Dan, his arms around his waist.

The balloon had stopped rising and, although it was still being carried along by the breeze, it was slowly sinking back to earth again.

'There are too many of us!' Agatha shouted, whilst the dog yapped and ran around her feet.

Beth held on to Dan and watched helplessly as he struggled to loose himself from the Ghost's grasp. They were drifting along as they descended, and Beth could see the ground rising up to meet them. Suddenly the snow covered field was replaced by a smooth white surface, like an ice-skating rink.

Beth only had a moment to realise that the hot air balloon had floated over a frozen lake, before the basket hit the surface with a crunch. She fell backwards, letting go of Dan's arms, beneath the force of the impact. Both Agatha and Franz stumbled too, but Franz managed to keep hold of Dan's arms.

'Agatha, *erhöhe die Flamme am*

Brenner!' Franz shouted over his shoulder, his hands digging into Dan's shirt as he held him in a tight grip.

They were being dragged along the surface of the frozen lake, the bottom edge of the basket kicking up shards of ice as they forged a path through the ice sheet. Beth felt like they had been thrown into a washing machine and the cycle set on spin as they were bounced and thrown around the confined space. The sound of crunching ice filled her head, along with the barking of the dog and Franz yelling at his wife.

The elderly German lady crawled over to the burner, but she couldn't manage to stay still long enough to get her hand on the control.

Beth groaned as she saw they were headed to the opposite side of the lake, whose shore was lined by another forest. If they couldn't get high enough in the next few seconds, the balloon would drive them straight into the trees. She wasn't sure how fast they were going, but she didn't like to think about the impact when the balloon smashed into the forest.

The Ghost was still clinging onto Dan's waist as they were dragged through the freezing water of the lake and bounced along the churning chunks of ice. Beth couldn't see how Dan could hang on for much longer.

Agatha managed to grab hold of the burner's controls. The flame whooshed and the balloon started rising again, lifting free of the frozen lake with a jolt. The dense mass of trees was approaching fast, a dark cliff face rushing to meet them and dash them to pieces.

With a loud cry Franz managed to drag Dan into the basket, his lower half soaked with freezing water, but free of the Ghost. The balloon was rising quickly now, and brushed through the top branches of the trees, cascading snow over everyone and almost extinguishing the propane flame.

But then they were free, soaring over the forest through a curtain of swirling snowflakes.

Dan collapsed on the floor, breathing hard. 'Thank you!' he gasped.

The dog jumped on Dan's chest and began licking his face. The woman lifted the dog off and scolded it. 'Oskar, *nein*!'

'He gets very excited,' Franz said. 'This is my wife, Agatha.'

Dan sat up, and as he did so Agatha placed a blanket around his shoulders. It seemed to Beth that she had an endless supply of checked blankets in her hamper.

'What happened to the Ghost?' Beth said.

Dan shook his head, trying to control his shakes. 'I don't know; he suddenly let go when the balloon started rising. I think he must have lost his grip.'

'Well, good riddance,' Agatha said, and huffed.

Dan looked up at Franz. 'We need to get to Paris, as quickly as possible.'

Beth gazed out of the basket as they floated higher and higher. She could see the warm glow of villages dotted around the countryside beneath her, and all around them the flurry of snow-flakes. After the excitement of being chased through the woods, she suddenly felt very peaceful.

'I am afraid we are at the mercy of the wind,' Franz said. 'The balloon takes us where the wind takes it.'

Dan sighed, and Beth suddenly saw the fight going out of him.

Franz smiled. 'But, fortunately, the wind is currently taking us to Paris.'

16

Beth and Dan sat huddled together beneath the two blankets, whilst Franz and Agatha bustled around fiddling with various parts of the burner and the basket. Oskar had curled up at their feet and appeared to be fast asleep. Beth wasn't entirely convinced he was asleep, though. Every now and then she noticed him opening one eye and looking at Dan, checking he was still there. The little dog seemed to have taken a liking to him.

'I always wanted to go on a romantic hot air balloon ride with you,' Beth said.

'I very much doubt this was what you had in mind though,' Dan replied, and gave her a smile. 'Still, we're here, together, and that's the most important thing.'

'How's your knee?'

'It hurts,' Dan replied. 'But I don't think he did any serious damage, just bruised it really.'

A silence fell between them. There seemed to be so much to say, and yet neither of them wanted to broach the subject.

'Beth,' Dan said finally, and then faltered and looked away for a moment.

'What is it?' Beth asked, although she wasn't sure she wanted to know the answer. Now that his memory had returned and he had realised that she knew what he did for a living, she wondered what his reaction would be. At the hotel he had been angry when he had seen her. Angry and dismissive. But now he obviously felt he had something important to say, and this was the first chance they'd had to be able to talk. What was he about to tell her? That he didn't love her anymore? Was he going to suggest that they should split up?

All these years he had been living a lie about the work that he did, about his professional life. But had their marriage been a true reflection of how he felt about her? Were all those times away with work, all those silences in the house, a way of him coping with the fact that he no longer loved her? If that was the case, if that was how he truly felt, then Beth knew she would have to accept that. Maybe it would be for the best. Once it was out in the open, perhaps she could move on, build a new life for herself. One that didn't involve loving a man who was never there for her.

Dan looked at her again, and there were tears in his eyes. 'Beth, I am so sorry,' he said. 'I'm sorry for all the lies, and I'm sorry for being away so often, and for leaving you with the kids. I know I have been a rotten husband these last few years, but it had to be that way.'

Beth took his hand and squeezed it, wanting to say something, to tell him that it was all right, that she loved him, but the words wouldn't come.

'I had to keep this part of my life a

secret from you and Toby and Sophie. I couldn't bear the thought of putting you in danger or causing you stress and worry every time I stepped out of our front door.' He wiped away his tears. 'At first it wasn't too bad, and I was able to juggle the responsibilities and the secrecy of work with family. But as the years passed, I felt like I was becoming two different people. The man I was at home grew more distant with every passing day, and I became scared that I was growing apart from you and the children.'

The basket creaked as they floated through the falling snow, over a landscape of white trees and fields and snow-covered farmhouses. Seeming to sense that Beth and Dan were having a heart to heart, Franz and Agatha kept their backs to them, giving them as much space as they could in the tiny basket.

'I had begun to think you didn't love me anymore,' Beth said. 'We drifted so far apart over the years, and I just thought it was part of married life, that this happened to everyone. And then I thought perhaps I could revitalise our marriage, bring some of the fun and excitement back into our relationship.'

'I know, I remember,' Dan said ruefully. 'But it was completely the wrong time, as that was when we first started suspecting there was a mole in the service. Everyone was on red alert, security was tightened, and the tension was unbelievable. Even I was suspected for a short while. Everyone was.'

'It must have been a terrible time for you, feeling all the stress at home whilst being under such pressure at work as well.'

'It wasn't easy,' Dan admitted. 'And to be honest, I was thinking that maybe I should get out of the business, give up the secret stuff, and spend more time at home. Become a regular person again, with no need for lies or secrets.'

'But you didn't,' Beth said.

Dan looked away again. He seemed to be struggling to compose himself.

'No,' he said finally. 'There are some very bad people out there in the world, Beth. And Section 13 does a lot of good work finding those people and stopping them from committing terrible crimes. I felt I had a responsibility to stay in the service, to play my part in bringing these criminals to justice, and helping to make the world a safer place, if only a little at least.'

'But what about your responsibility to Sophie and Toby? They need their father, Dan.'

'I know.' Dan turned to face her again, and this time she could see the lines of tears down his cheeks. 'But you've got to understand, it was because of Sophie and Toby that I decided against quitting my job. I don't want them growing up in a world where violence is the norm; where they see dreadful deeds committed for some obscure ideology, played out on the news every night.'

Beth cuddled up to her husband a little closer. 'You can't solve all the world's problems by yourself, Dan.

'I know.'

'But you can make a difference in our children's lives by being there for them — by being a constant presence in their days and their weeks, in the months and the years that they have left of growing up. Maybe you can't make the world a better place for them, but you can help continue to make them into better people, and help them forge their own identities as good, strong, loving adults.'

Dan wiped at his eyes. 'When we get back home, I'll contact Tamara. I'll tell them I intend to resign from the service.'

'That would be nice,' Beth said, and smiled.

'I love you, Beth,' Dan said, and leaned over and kissed her lightly on the lips.

'I love you too,' she whispered.

'Paris is up ahead,' Franz shouted, his voice loud in the cold night air.

Beth and Dan both struggled to their feet. She felt as though she had been pummelled and punched and thrown off a moving train, her body ached so much. They stood with Franz and Agatha, and looked where he pointed. Through the swirling eddies of snow, Beth could see the warm orange glow of the city lights and the multicoloured beacon that was the Eiffel Tower at Christmas.

'It's beautiful,' she whispered.

'Can't we go any faster?' Dan asked, turning to Franz and gripping the edge of the basket.

Franz shrugged. 'We can only go as fast as the wind carries us. We will be there soon.'

'Dan?' Beth said, her stomach growing tight with anxiety.

'We haven't got much time,' he said. 'Sean told me there are explosives planted at the north and west pillars, using the same physics as when old buildings get destroyed. Remember when we watched the old multi-storey car park being taken down last summer? How it just collapsed in on itself?'

Beth nodded.

'That's because the explosive devices were planted at the base of the building. With the supporting structures blown apart, the building just collapsed in on itself. This is slightly different. Parker has planted a specialist explosive called RDX at the base of the north and west pillars. RDX is particularly powerful, and when ignited will slice right through the iron latticework. The tower will then be left standing on only two legs, and it will topple over, just like a person would if he had one leg kicked out from under him. The Eiffel Tower is three hundred meters high. If the Order succeed in toppling it, not only will the people on the tower and those in the immediate area die, but there will be a great deal of death and destruction in the surrounding area, especially to the northwest.'

'Can you defuse them?' Beth said.

'Yes,' Dan replied, looking grim. 'I need to remove the fuse from the blasting cap. Once I've done that, the RDX is harmless.'

'That's good then. We can stop this. Can't we?'

'I've got to find the explosives first. And I've got to do it before they are detonated. My gut feeling is that they won't be wired up to a timer. Somebody will be nearby, able to prime and ignite the fuse with a radio or mobile device.'

'Parker?'

Dan nodded. 'My guess is he will be somewhere nearby, but far enough away that he won't get caught in the fallout when the tower collapses. He'll be waiting until he feels that the crowds are thick enough that he will cause maximum damage.'

'But surely that could be any time now?' Beth cried.

Dan looked anxiously at Beth. He didn't need to say anything. They were running out of time — and if they didn't get to the Eiffel Tower soon, or if the wind changed direction and took them off course, then thousands of people were going to die.

17

Franz adjusted the controls on the propane burner, reducing the intensity of the flame, and the balloon began descending. Oskar the dog ran around in circles, barking excitedly.

Beth gazed out of the basket at a vista of golden, twinkling lights. She could see car headlights moving steadily along the roads; boats cruising along the river Seine, bright with colourful lights in contrast to the dark water; and the monuments of Paris bathed in blue and gold. It seemed as though she must be dreaming, floating over night-time Paris in winter, snow falling all around them. If only they weren't racing against time to try and avert a terrible catastrophe, she would be able to enjoy the magical sensation of flying, and the beautiful city below.

'Where are you going to land?' Dan shouted.

'We will land in the Champs de Mars,' Franz replied, staring intently ahead.

'You can't!' Dan shouted. 'It will be full of people — a huge crowd of thousands gathering around the Eiffel Tower for the Midnight Mass.'

Franz shrugged. 'It is perfect for landing our balloon: a large, flat area. There is nowhere else.'

'But what about all the people gathered for the Mass?' Beth said.

Franz shrugged again. 'They will have to move.'

Dan gave Beth a tight, worried smile. They were trying to save lives, not kill people by squashing them.

As the balloon descended, its rate of speed decreased. The Eiffel Tower was drawing close now, and Beth could see the crowds filling the Champs de Mars. A stage had been set up at the base of the tower and a huge Christmas tree stood to one side, lit up with twinkling Christmas lights and decorations.

Had anyone seen the hot air balloon

approaching them yet? Did nobody realise the danger they were in? Franz had turned off the propane burner now, and without the roar of the flame, they were floating silently towards the gathered crowd.

Beth was thinking about yelling, screaming at people to get out of the way, to run, when a series of honks startled her. Franz was leaning over the edge of the basket with an old-fashioned brass car horn. He was squeezing the rubber bulb, the brass horn honking at the crowd below. Faces turned upwards to see where the noise was coming from.

It was only a matter of seconds before people were yelling and scream-ing, and the crowd started dispersing as they tried to get out of the way.

'There, what did I tell you?' Franz shouted, laughing as he gleefully honked the car horn. 'They will move, I said — and look at them. They are moving!'

Causing a panic, more like, Beth thought. *Someone's going to get hurt down there.*

But if they didn't get down on the ground and defuse the bombs set to explode at the base of the Eiffel Tower, the alternative was a lot, lot worse.

Oskar was still running around in circles and barking. Agatha placed a comforting arm around Beth's shoulders. 'Get ready,' she said. 'You need to hold onto something; we are about to land.'

Beth and Dan both grabbed onto the lip of the basket. Franz was still leaning over the edge, honking the car horn, laughing. Agatha had hold of a cord leading up into the envelope, as the balloon was called. She had told Beth that the cord was connected to a small parachute over a hole at the apex of the balloon, which helped control its descent. Just before they touched the ground, Agatha was going to pull the parachute into the balloon, letting the envelope deflate rapidly and prevent them from being dragged along the ground.

They hit the ground with a crash, much more of an abrupt landing than Beth had been expecting, and all of the balloon's occupants fell over. Oskar leapt on top of Beth, barking excitedly, and Franz was lying on his back, still honking the horn and laughing.

Before Beth had struggled to her feet, disoriented and sore, the basket had been surrounded by an angry mob cursing at them in French and waving their fists.

Franz leapt to his feet, remarkably nimble for an old man, still honking his brass horn, and shouted in French, 'Out of the way! The balloon, it is deflating!'

The envelope was like a huge jellyfish, slowly floating down and expanding as the hot air rapidly cooled. The crowd began scattering again, screaming and yelling and trying to run beyond its reach before it settled on top of them like a heavy blanket.

Dan climbed out of the basket and began running towards the Eiffel Tower, lit up with Christmas lights, a beacon against the night sky. Beth jumped out of the basket and followed him; and, with an excited bark, so did Oskar.

Dan sprinted through the crowd, his feet kicking up clouds of white, powdery snow. Beth's lungs were aching with the effort of running and her chest throbbed as she sucked in cold air. No matter how hard she ran, the distance between her and Dan increased, and soon she had lost him amongst the people in their thick winter jackets, scarves and hats. Despite the cold, Beth was sweating, and she knew that when she stopped running she would grow increasingly chilled. But she had to try and keep up with Dan. At least she had the Eiffel Tower to guide her.

Oskar ran beside her, barking and wagging his tail.

Beth had to stop running, leaning her hands on her knees as she took a breather. Oskar ran around her feet, barking and leaping up and down.

'All right, all right,' Beth gasped. 'Just give me a moment, will you?'

Taking another ragged breath, she

straightened up and began running again. The tower loomed over her, much larger than she had ever realised. She had completely lost Dan now, and couldn't even begin to think how to locate him. Where had he said the bombs were located? The north and west pillars.

But which was north and which was west?

Beth slowed to a halt and cried out in frustration. She had no idea how to start looking for the explosive devices, and even less of an idea what to do with one if she found it.

Dan was on his own now.

But perhaps that was for the best.

As Beth had only recently found out, this was what he did.

It was his job.

18

Parker pushed his way through the crowds. He had a bad feeling in the pit of his stomach, and as much as he was trying to convince himself it was because of a dodgy burger he had bought from a street vendor half an hour earlier, he knew it wasn't.

Now was the time to detonate the explosives and send the tower toppling to the ground like a child's pillar of wooden blocks, but with much more devastating results. The first thing he had to do, though, was get well clear of the blast zone. How ironic it would be if he died in what tomorrow's newspapers would surely be calling a Christmas tragedy, without ever collecting his big fat payday. His reward from the Order of Omicron. Parker had no interest in their ideologies or their religious beliefs. As far as he was concerned they were a bunch of crazies. All he was interested in was the money they were paying him.

But that bad feeling was growing worse, and he needed to finish the plan and detonate those explosives now.

Because, although he was convinced that Dan and that silly wife of his couldn't be here, seeing that hot air balloon land on the Champs de Mars had unnerved him.

Parker had put enough Rohypnol in their coffees; they might still be asleep now. The service station had been closing down for Christmas Day, and Parker had got himself a key for a room in the motel and stowed Dan and Beth in there. With no car and no transport available, they should be stuck there still, helpless to do anything, even if Dan's memory had returned.

Parker should have just killed them.

That would have been the simple solution.

But Parker and Dan went back a long way. They'd been out in the field together, they'd cracked cases together and, most significantly, Dan had saved Parker's life. So Parker felt he owed Dan one. As much as he would have liked to take the simple route, he couldn't bring himself to do it. And so he'd spent the last couple of days chasing around Paris trying to get Dan and Beth out of the way of that freak the Ghost, away from Tamara Peel and her goons from Section 13, and somewhere they couldn't interfere with the plan.

Parker liked Dan. They'd had some good times together on the job. Parker couldn't really pin down when the money had started becoming more important than his principles, or how the Order had insinuated themselves in his life. But he knew that once the Eiffel Tower had collapsed and it was all over the news worldwide, he was going to receive a huge sum of money in a safe bank account in Thailand.

And then Parker was going to disappear. Forever.

But still . . . That hot air balloon, floating down from the sky thick with snow; that old guy leaning out of the basket and honking on that old-fashioned car horn. Crazy old guy, that's all it was.

Dan and Beth couldn't be involved with that.

No way.

Parker pushed on through the crowds, heading for his safe spot across the Pont d'Iena onto the Place de Varsovie on the opposite bank of the Seine.

And then he could push that button on his cell phone and safely watch the destruction of one of the world's most iconic structures.

Sweet.

★   ★   ★

Dan ran toward the north pillar, shoving people out of his way, yelling at them to move, move, *move!*

There was no time for being polite; he had to defuse those bombs before they were detonated. His contact, Sean, had been unsure as to whether or not they were timer activated or manual, but that didn't matter anymore. What Dan knew for certain was that they could go off at any moment. He just wished that he hadn't got Beth involved, or the old couple in their balloon. At least they were on the south-facing aspect of the tower and, if the worst happened, they should be relatively safe.

Dan reached the north pillar, the ticket office at its base, a line of people snaking from it between the metal barriers. He leapt over the first barrier and elbowed his way through the line, then jumped over the next barrier.

A large woman shouted at him and someone else protested. Climbing onto a rubbish bin, Dan hoisted himself onto the snow-covered canopy over the ticket office. He was in amongst the iron latticework of the pillar now, and he turned slowly on the spot, head arched back as he searched for anything out of the ordinary.

There, in amongst the shadows, tucked into a corner where two of the girders met at a joint, Dan could see a tiny blue light. Where it was positioned there was no way it could be seen from the ground, and it was only because Dan was standing on the ticket office roof that he had found it. Wires led down from the small black box attached to the ironwork, across the edge of the ticket office roof, and then to the sticks of RDX explosive hidden in the ironwork of the supporting structure.

Dan reached up and carefully pulled at the black box. After some initial resistance it came away from the iron girder, the wires that snaked from its side coming with it. He looked at the blue light, glowing steadily. Didn't look like any kind of timer device that he had ever come across. He turned it over.

The back was a simple slide-and-click cover, like the covers on battery compartments on travel clocks and children's toys. Dan slid the cover off and dropped it on the ticket office roof. The mechanism was a basic electric circuit. A SIM card had been inserted into the device. Parker obviously had a mobile phone and, when he was ready, would dial the number for the SIM card, activating a tiny power surge. That power surge would then send an electrical current through the wires to the blasting caps on the RDX. Once ignited, the RDX-based explosive compounds would expand at a very high rate of speed, up to 27,000 feet per second, and the concentrated, high-velocity pressure would slice right through the iron, splitting it in half.

Dan wound the wires around his fist and then yanked them from the black box.

With the electrical circuit permanently broken, the RDX was harmless.

Now to find the second device.

★ ★ ★

Beth approached the base of one of the tower's pillars, Oskar trotting by her side. She had tried shooing him away and telling him to go back to Franz and Agatha, but with no success. He had decided he was sticking with her and, although she was concerned about losing him in the crowd, there was nothing she could do about it.

'Just stay close, okay?' she said.

Oskar wagged his tail and barked his agreement.

Up close the tower looked just as beautiful, bathed in the glow from lights projected on its latticework. She tilted her head back and gazed up at the beam of light projected from the top, like a searchlight roaming over Paris. Flakes of cold snow drifted gently down onto her face.

What am I doing? There's no way I can find Dan now; and even if I did, what use would I be? I would be more of a hindrance than a help.

She wondered how serious he had been when he had said that he intended to leave Section 13. After all the years of subterfuge, could he really settle down into an ordinary, nine-to-five job? It seemed to Beth that, once they were safely home again, Dan might begin to regret his decision to retire from the secret service. Life at home, in a semi-detached with two children and an elderly cat, was going to be no competition for travelling around the world fighting bad guys, surely? And how could she compete with glamorous colleagues such as Tamara Peel?

If Tamara were here, she would know exactly what to do. She would know which was north, and which was west, and she would battle her way through the crowds with determination, and be by Dan's side as he defused the bombs.

What could Beth offer him? A detailed account of her day at work, teaching unruly six-year-olds? A pile of dirty washing that needed putting in the washing machine, and a bathroom that needed cleaning?

Could Dan actually cope with the banal reality of everyday life, in contrast to the thrill of his job as an operative for Section 13?

Oskar barked, obviously wondering why they had stopped running. Beth knelt down and ruffled his head. 'Come on, little guy,' she said sadly. 'Let's get you back to your owners.'

She stood up — and her heart jumped a beat, and began pounding hard.

She had glimpsed a man in the crowd, his back to her, wearing a parka, the hood up. A flake of snow fell on her eyelid; she blinked it away, and the man was gone. Could it have been him? Was he here to stop Dan from defusing the explosive devices?

'Oskar, stay with me,' she said. 'Looks like we're going Ghost-hunting.'

19

Dan scrambled through the crowds, running as hard as he could, shoving his way past men, women, and children. Franz and his hot air balloon landing in the middle of the Champs de Mars had had an unexpected benefit. All the security guards had rushed over there to investigate the bizarre appearance of a hot air balloon, leaving Dan free to barge his way to the front of the queues and climb on top of the ticket offices.

He arrived at the west pillar. How long did he have left? Was Parker even now readying his mobile device, depressing the button that would send the signal to activate the electrical charge, the current running through the wires to the blasting caps, which would then ignite the RDX? With one set of explosive devices made safe, Dan wondered how long the Eiffel Tower could remain standing on three pillars if the second one exploded.

Not long, surely. The added stress on the remaining three support columns would be too much. Even if it didn't topple over straight away, it wouldn't be long before the ironwork began to shift and twist; before joints began to shear apart and the pillars ripped free of their foundations.

Dan jumped over the first metal barrier, pushing his way through the queue of people, and climbed over the next one.

A huge man with a Yankee baseball cap perched on his head blocked his path. The man was breathing heavily, the rolls of fat around his neck hiding his chin, so that it seemed his face just disappeared into his chest.

'Whaddayathinkyerdoin?' he rasped.

'You need to let me past,' Dan said.

He tried dodging past him, but despite his massive bulk and an apparent breathing problem, he moved fast and blocked Dan's way.

'Yagottajointhendofthequeue,' he wheezed.

'No, you don't understand,' Dan replied.

He took a step back and bumped into someone behind. Everyone was staring at him, this queue-jumper who expected to be let in to the ticket office without having to wait. Dan had no time for this; he needed to get on the roof of the ticket office, beneath the west pillar, and look for the RDX, and for the device that would ignite it. But neither could he fight his way past these people. He didn't want to hurt them, and one wrong blow to the big guy, who was a heart attack waiting to happen, could end up killing him.

A disturbance further up the queue behind Dan distracted everyone. There was a scream, the clatter of one of the metal barriers being pushed over, and then another scream. People were moving, trying to get away, men yelling, more screams.

'Your lives are in danger!' Dan shouted, his eyes fixed on the point where the screams were coming from. 'You need to leave — now!'

No one moved, and the fat man stood his ground, wheezing.

The crowd in front of Dan parted and the Ghost stepped through, his hood pulled back to reveal his white plastic face, his lips peeled away from his diamond-studded teeth in a ghastly approximation of a smile.

* * *

Parker found himself a bench on the Place de Varsovie with a good view of the Eiffel Tower. He brushed the snow off the seat and sat down.

Paris, he had to admit, looked stunning at night, and the Eiffel Tower was its crowning achievement — the iconic European monument to beat them all. The lights lit it up beautifully; and the spotlight on top, roaming over the city sky like the Bat Signal summoning Batman, was a nice, dramatic touch.

Such a shame that in just a few moments from now it was going to be reduced to a twisted, smoking pile of iron.

Parker pulled the cheap mobile phone out of his pocket.

Not even Batman could stop him now.

He switched the phone on and let it boot up. There was no hurry. Dan and Beth were safely ensconced in a motorway service station motel, and nobody else had a single idea about what was going to happen tonight.

Except . . . there was that hot air balloon landing on the Champs de Mars. That was still bothering Parker. He didn't see how it could have been anything to do with Dan and Beth, but it had been an unusual event to say the least. And Parker didn't like it when the unexpected happened. Surprises, he had learnt over the years, were never good.

The cell phone's welcome screen lit up, and Parker opened up the on-screen keypad. He punched in a number he had committed to memory several weeks ago, and then his thumb hovered over the green telephone icon. Now that he had come to the moment of truth, he found he was hesitating.

But why?

All he had to do was activate the call with a single touch of his thumb on the screen and, seconds later, he would see and hear the explosion from across the river.

Parker closed his eyes.

Think of the money.

His thumb touched the screen, and the telephone icon turned red.

20

Beth screamed at the sound of the explosion and instinctively ducked.

Someone laughed, and when Beth straightened up she realised there had been no explosion. The sound had been one of the metal barriers that helped herd people into an orderly queue falling over and crashing to the ground. Her nerves were like fishing wire stretched taut, ready to snap at the nearest pull.

And she had lost the Ghost.

Oskar barked, looking up eagerly at her. From his expression he seemed to be wondering why they had stopped again, and where were they going next.

'I don't know, little fella,' she said. 'What do you think? Any ideas?'

Beth headed for the spot where she had last seen the Ghost. She was close to the base of one of the pillars now, but she didn't know if it was north, west, south or east. There was some kind of commotion ahead, and then the sound of another metal barrier crashing to the ground. The crowd before her pushed back in a ripple effect, people stepping out of the way of something.

Curious, Beth pushed her way through to see what the disturbance was.

Dan and the Ghost stood facing each other. They looked as though they had already been fighting, and were now at some kind of stalemate. Two of the metal barriers lay on the ground, in the snow. Was the Ghost trying to stop Dan getting to one of the explosive devices? If so, he was on a suicide mission, and he would stop at nothing to keep Dan from defusing those bombs, even if it cost him his own life.

There was a bright flash, and Beth realised that several people were holding up their mobile phones, taking pictures. She grabbed the mobile phone off a man standing next to her and ran up behind the Ghost. As she expected, he turned at the sound of her approach.

She held the phone up in front of his eyes and took a photograph.

The Ghost reeled as the powerful flash dazzled him. Beth had only a moment to exult in her small victory before he had blindly lashed out and knocked her to the ground.

In a frenzy of barking and growling, Oskar flew at the Ghost and sank his teeth into the assassin's leg. The Ghost kicked him away and advanced upon Beth, lying on her back in the snow.

★　★　★

Parker stood up, clutching the mobile phone, unable to believe what his eyes were telling him. There had been no explosion, and the Eiffel Tower was still standing, its spotlight piercing the snow-filled air. What had happened? Had he punched in the wrong number?

His hands shaking, he tried the number on the phone again, and clicked connect. He stared into the distance, waiting for that first explosion.

Nothing.

It was Dan — it had to be. He had found the bomb and defused it. Parker's instincts had been correct. Somehow, maybe in that hot air balloon that had caused such a disturbance, Dan had made his way back to the centre of Paris. Which meant his memory had returned, too, and he would know all about Parker now, and the plot to destroy the Eiffel Tower.

Parker bunched his hands into fists and swore. If that tower didn't come down, then he wasn't going to get paid, and all of this had been for nothing. He would be on the run for the rest of his life.

He held the mobile phone up in front of his face and stared at the glowing screen. His only hope was that Dan hadn't found the second set of RDX yet. With another SIM card inside the trigger device, that was on another number. Setting up two of the tower's pillars to be damaged by explosions had been Parker's way of ensuring the job got done. But one pillar should be enough. It might take a little longer for the stress to build up in the iron latticework when the tower was standing on three feet, but the end result would be the same, and it would topple to the ground.

Parker keyed in the new number on the phone, and this time he didn't hesitate to hit the green telephone icon, smiling as it turned red. He put the phone to his ear and waited for it to connect.

*   *   *

It ripped Dan's heart apart to leave Beth at the mercy of the Ghost, but he knew that if he didn't find that second explosive device and defuse it, they would all be dead. He ran for the tower entrance, climbing up the frontage and onto the roof. A security guard, possibly the only one who hadn't gone running over to investigate the bizarre and unexpected appearance of a hot air balloon at a Christmas Mass, shouted at Dan.

Dan ignored him. Now he was

directly under the pillar, and he scanned the iron latticework, searching for the blue light that he had found in the north pillar.

There!

He reached up and pulled the black box from the girder. No need to open this one up; he knew exactly how it worked. Bunching the wires up in his fist, Dan took a good hold of them and yanked.

The wires pulled free of the black box, just as the blue light turned red.

Dan sank down to his knees on the roof, thick with snow, and let the wires and the black box fall from his hands.

They were safe.

And then Beth screamed.

★ ★ ★

Parker stared at the Eiffel Tower, willing it to collapse in a screech of tangled iron. But the tower obstinately remained standing, showing no signs of stress, or explosions at its base.

The RDX had been deactivated.

And Parker was a dead man.

The Order of Omicron weren't going to stand by and let such a massive failure go unpunished. If he didn't get moving fast, that freak they called the Ghost would be after him. Parker had to run, and keep on running for the rest of his life.

The first thing to do would be to go back to his room and grab the briefcase full of euros. That was only supposed to be the down payment, but after Parker's catastrophic failure in bringing down the Eiffel Tower there would be no money transferred to his account. The cash in the briefcase wasn't going to last him long, but hopefully it would get him out of the country and keep him on the run for a couple of months at least.

Parker lobbed the mobile into the Seine and watched as it plunged through the thin layer of soft ice on top of the moving water. Best not leave any evidence at the scene, if he could help it.

With one last look at the Eiffel Tower,

perhaps hoping that it might suddenly collapse in a plume of flames and smoke, Parker turned to make his exit.

And came face to face with a gun pointed at his head.

'Turn around and put your hands on your head,' Tamara Peel said.

Parker stared at her, unable to believe his eyes. She held the gun out at arm's length, and she was standing with her feet planted shoulder-width apart, dressed in her usual attire of dark trouser suit and white shirt open at the collar. She looked like she meant business.

Parker hated her.

Behind Tamara were three more agents, all with guns trained on him.

Parker sighed, placed his hands on his head and turned around.

'Okay, Tomato Peel,' he said. 'Do your worst.'

21

Beth screamed as the Ghost lunged at her, snapping his diamond-studded teeth like a hungry dog. Dan was on the roof of the ticket office, looking for the bomb. He couldn't help her. And everybody else had backed up at the sight of the Ghost, his terrifying appearance frightening them off.

Oskar leapt on the assassin again, growling and barking, and sank his teeth into his thigh. The Ghost fell over and rolled onto his back. He grabbed the dog by the scruff of the neck and threw him away. Oskar squealed in pain or fear, Beth wasn't sure, as he hit the ground and rolled over in a white cloud of snow.

Beth turned and ran blindly, pushing her way through the people blocking her in. She realised she was in the entrance, the iron steps ahead leading up the pillar to the first floor. Hearing people scream behind her, and knowing that she had nowhere else to go, Beth ran for the steps and started climbing.

The Champ de Mars and the surrounding area of Paris began receding below Beth as she ran up the staircase. Clinging onto the handrail, she began pulling herself up as her thighs and calf muscles started burning with the effort of running. She was quickly out of breath, and promised herself that she would start going to the gym as soon as she returned to England.

The staircase kept switching back on itself, causing her head to swim as she became disorientated, always having to swing left at the top of every flight. The metallic thudding of her shoes on the iron steps filled her head like a band of drummers, pounding out the same rhythm over and over and over.

After what seemed like an age, Beth stumbled onto the first-floor viewing platform. If she'd had time — if she hadn't been so panicked by the thought of the Ghost chasing her, or wracked with anxiety at the thought that Dan hadn't disabled the explosive devices — she would have stopped to enjoy the view.

Paris stretched out before her like something from a film set. The orange and yellow glow of lights punctured the night, whilst snow continued falling gently from the dark sky. It was a Christmas scene like no other, but Beth didn't have time to enjoy it. The Ghost had appeared on the platform, just like the apparition he was named after. He stared at her with dark eyes, in contrast to his white face, and pulled his lips back in a frightening approximation of a smile.

'Help me, please,' Beth gasped, grabbing the arm of a man next to her.

'What the . . . ?' he blurted out when he saw the Ghost approaching.

Other people on the viewing platform were already backing away. The Ghost strode towards Beth, never taking his eyes off her. It seemed as though he had forgotten about Dan, and about the plot to destroy the Eiffel Tower. He only seemed to have one thing in mind now — and that was to capture and kill Beth.

'In the restaurant, quick,' the man said, pushing her towards the glass-fronted double doors. 'I used to be in the army. I can sort this joker out.'

Beth pushed through the doors, into the warmth of the restaurant. Couples in smart dress were seated at tables covered in white tablecloths. Many of them looked up curiously at Beth, her hair tangled, eyes wide with fear, and face flushed from all the running up the stairs. One woman shook her head and tutted at the state of Beth's clothes and her casual attire.

A waiter rushed over, speaking in rapid French, but Beth ignored him. She was watching, through the larger window, the Ghost approaching her rescuer. The fight was brief and brutal, and Beth cried out as the man fell beneath the onslaught of the Ghost's attack. The assassin turned his head and looked directly at her as she stood inside the restaurant.

Beth turned and ran, dodging between tables, ignoring the shouts of annoyance and anger as she banged into tables, spilled glasses of wine, and upset plates of food. Barging through another set of double doors, she found herself back on the viewing platform. She saw the lift for the next floor, and the stairs.

She took the stairs, running up them as fast as her exhausted legs would carry her. Behind and below her, she heard more screams and the crash of upturned tables.

The Ghost was on his way.

Again Beth found herself running up a seemingly endless flight of iron steps, surrounded by the latticework structure of one of the Eiffel Tower's pillars. At the top of each flight of steps she swung herself around a corner, using the handrail to steady herself, and began the ascent to the next corner. She passed tourists coming down but simply pushed past them, with no idea of where she was going or what she was going to do if she got to the top.

All she could do was run on instinct.

At the second floor, Beth tripped and fell. A young couple stepped forward to help her, and then stepped back again. Beth didn't need to look behind her to see why. There was no point in trying to run anymore. She had been stupid to run into the Eiffel Tower. There was nowhere left to go, except up to the top — where she would be trapped.

She cried out as strong hands grabbed her and rolled her over. The Ghost leered at her, his dark eyes glittering like precious stones set in a plastic facemask. He lifted her up like she was a rag doll. Beth didn't have the strength to fight back.

'Please,' she said, her voice a tired croak. 'What have I done, why are you doing this?'

The Ghost stared at her, his face a stiff, blank mask, and his black eyes like deep, empty holes.

Why doesn't he speak? she thought weakly. *Why doesn't he say anything, anything at all?*

The Ghost bared his teeth, and up close Beth could see how sharp they were, filed down to points like a shark's. She closed her eyes, too weak to fight back, helpless in this monster's grip.

'Put her down.'

Dan stepped out of the elevator. He had a gun trained on the Ghost. Tamara Peel followed him, also with a gun.

The Ghost smiled, the diamonds glittering in the lights. He let go of Beth, who stumbled and fell backwards, landing on her bottom, just like she had when she first met Tamara Peel at the hotel.

'Put your hands on your head and turn around,' Tamara said.

The Ghost didn't move, but stared at Tamara and Dan like he was considering his options. Two men in dark suits appeared at the top of the stairs. They also had guns, and they pointed them at the Ghost.

Finally, the assassin did as he was told, and he was quickly handcuffed. The two agents escorted him to the lift.

Dan rushed over to Beth and helped her up, enveloping her in a huge hug. The relief of knowing she was safe, of having Dan back, and being held by him in his strong arms, overwhelmed her.

'I thought I'd lost you,' he whispered, holding her tight, his warm breath feathering her cheek.

Beth held onto him as though, if she let go, she might fall and lose him forever.

'Is it over?' she asked. 'Did you defuse the bombs?'

'Yes, we're safe. Everyone's safe,' Dan replied. 'And Parker has been caught, too. It's all over, Beth.'

'Oh, thank God,' she gasped.

'I'm sorry to break up the reunion,' Tamara said, all business as usual, 'but I think we should get you down, and somewhere warm. We need to debrief you both, get statements, and start processing this through the system.'

Dan pulled away from Beth. She tried to cling onto him, but he gently prised her hands away. 'Wait here,' he said.

He took Tamara by the elbow and guided her away, their backs to Beth. She watched them as they talked quietly, and a pang of jealousy shot through her chest. Beth told herself to stop being silly.

But still, what were they talking about?

Finally they both turned around, and Tamara smiled. Beth was amazed at how much that smile transformed her face and softened her features.

'We'll see you down on the ground, then. Don't be too long.'

Beth looked questioningly at Dan as he took her hand and led her to the lift.

'What's going on?' she asked.

'You'll find out,' Dan replied.

The view of Paris from the glass-sided elevator was amazing. The snow had stopped falling, and the whole city was laid out before them as they rose ever higher. Beth felt like she was flying; and with Dan's arm around her shoulders, and hers around his waist, she was suddenly the happiest woman alive.

The elevator took them to the top of the Eiffel Tower. They stepped out onto the viewing platform and took in the view once more, holding each other, not speaking.

After the hectic pace of the last few days, they appreciated the quiet. For the moment, nothing needed to be said.

Eventually, Dan pulled himself away. 'Wait here,' he said.

Beth gave him a puzzled look but said nothing. She turned back to the view. For a brief moment she had a vision of the explosives slicing the supporting pillars apart, and of the tower toppling, and she shuddered. But then it passed, and Beth took a deep breath, reminding herself that she was safe.

They all were.

When she turned back around, Dan

was approaching her with a glass of champagne in each hand. Behind him she could see the champagne bar.

'What's this for?' she asked.

Dan laughed. 'I'm supposed to be the one with the memory problems!' He gave her a glass, and they clinked them together. 'Happy anniversary, darling.'

Realisation dawned, and Beth smiled. 'Of course! It's Christmas Eve!'

They both took a sip of the cold, sparkling champagne, and then kissed.

Dan smiled. 'I always said I would take you up the Eiffel Tower one day, and that we would kiss at the very top, overlooking the most romantic city in the world.'

Beth laughed. 'You didn't have to involve the secret service and a pasty-faced assassin with dental problems, though. You could have just asked me.'

Dan opened his mouth to reply, but they were both distracted by the sound of a car horn honking repeatedly. When they turned towards the noise, looking out over the Parisian cityscape, they saw the German couple's colourful hot air balloon rising up and filling their field of vision. Franz and Agatha, standing in the basket, waved furiously, and Franz continued to honk the brass car horn. Oskar, who was being held tightly by Agatha, barked happily.

'You have a romantic holiday now, yes?' Franz shouted, laughing.

'Yes! Thank you!' Beth shouted back.

'God bless you both!' Agatha cried, as the balloon rose higher and began drifting away.

'Goodbye!' Dan shouted, waving.

'Goodbye, Oskar!' Beth cried out.

They watched as the balloon drifted over the city and away, listening to Franz honking the brass horn, and Oskar barking.

'Where do you think they're headed?' Dan said.

'Wherever the wind takes them,' Beth replied wistfully.

Eventually, when they could hear them no longer and the balloon was just a tiny dot in the night sky, Beth turned back to Dan and sank her head against his chest, then wrapped her arms around his waist.

'Dan?' she said, wearily.

'Hmm?'

'Can we go home now?'

22

Back home in England, Christmas Day passed in a flurry of presents, roast turkey with all the trimmings, drinks, laughter, games, Christmas TV, and lots of sitting down with groans of having eaten too much. Sophie and Toby were delighted to have their mum and dad back for Christmas and, with Sara, they all spent Christmas Day at Beth's parents' house.

'The two of you look very happy together,' Sara said to Beth when they had a moment together.

They were in the kitchen, tackling the first round of washing-up after Christmas dinner. Beth had been nagging her parents for years to buy themselves a dishwasher (or a 'washing-up machine', as Beth's mother called them) but they refused. That was all too newfangled for them.

'We are,' Beth replied, smiling.

Sara handed Beth a dripping plate. 'So come on, tell me all about your trip to Paris. How did Dan react when he first saw you at the hotel?'

Beth wiped the plate and stacked it with the others, thinking back to that moment when Dan had first seen her. 'Well, he was very surprised.'

'I'll bet he was! And then what did you do?'

'We went for a drive,' Beth said, taking another plate from Sara.

Sara paused for a moment, resting her hands on the edge of the sink, a faraway look coming over her. 'A nice romantic drive around Paris — how wonderful! I bet that's when you had your heart to heart with him, wasn't it?'

'That's right,' Beth replied, thinking back to the argument they'd had as Dan sped the car through the Paris streets, chasing the Ghost.

'Did you visit anywhere in Paris?'

Well, I was chased through the Cata-combs, a network of tunnels beneath

311

Paris, the walls of which are lined with skeletons. We went to a cathedral where we fought an assassin called the Ghost. Then we attended a Father Christmas convention where I had to dress up as Mrs Christmas. Then we were chased through a forest, before we went for a hot air balloon ride over the city with a wonderfully bonkers German couple and their dog Oskar. Finally, I was chased up the Eiffel Tower by the Ghost, who was trying to kill me.

'Oh no, not really. We just sort of stayed in our room, mainly,' Beth said.

'Don't tell me any more,' Sara said, a mischievous glint in her eyes.

'How's it all going in here?' Dan asked, entering the kitchen. 'Can I help?'

'Actually, we were just going to take a break from the washing up and have a cup of tea,' Beth said.

'Beth has been telling me all about your romantic break in Paris!' Sara said, drying her hands.

Dan raised an eyebrow. 'Oh?'

'Don't worry, Mr Bond, your secret is safe,' Sara said. She flicked the towel at Dan and laughed. 'She didn't give away any details.'

'What was that all about?' Dan asked when Sara had gone into the living room to take orders for drinks and slices of Christmas cake.

Beth smiled. 'Don't worry, I gave her the impression that we spent the whole time in our hotel room.'

'But what about the James Bond comment?'

She laughed. 'It's that habit you have of raising one eyebrow when you're confused. Remember your Roger Moore impersonation that reduced all those Mrs Christmases to mountains of wobbling jelly?'

'I'd forgotten all about that.'

'Hmph,' Beth snorted in mock outrage. 'I've been doing my best to try and forget. Now stop worrying; Sara doesn't know a thing.'

'Good. You know we can't ever tell them about my job, or what really went on in Paris, don't you?'

Beth gave Dan a swift dig in the ribs, and he yelped. 'Of course I do. Your secrets are safe with me, Mr Bond.'

Dan wrapped his arms around her and pulled her close. 'You do realise that James Bond isn't just a famous spy, but that he has other areas of expertise too, don't you?'

Beth returned the hug. 'Oh yes? What would those be then?'

'Well, I do seem to remember that he is quite the ladies' man.'

'I do hope that is 'lady's man' in the singular and not the plural, Mr Bond. I'd hate to think that you ever got up close and personal with another woman whilst on a job.'

'Hmm, no. Tomatoes don't agree with me, if I'm honest. Ouch!' Beth had delivered another sharp dig in his side.

'You know, thinking about Tomato Peel, that reminds me — why did she have that briefcase full of euros with her when she found us at the inn?'

'The money was a down payment from the Order for Parker. Once the Eiffel Tower had been destroyed, they were going to transfer a much bigger sum into a bank account for him, and he was going to disappear forever. Tamara had searched his hotel room and found the money, then came straight to collect us and take us somewhere safe.'

'But how did she know where we were?'

'One of her men tailed us. No one was entirely sure what we were up to at first, and it wasn't until I stole the money off Tamara and we escaped that she realised how bad my memory loss was.'

'I was so scared, being chased through Paris by all sorts of people, with my husband who had no memory of anything at all,' Beth said, hugging him again. 'Remember what you said to me in the hot air balloon? Were you serious about giving up working for Section 13?'

'Yes, I was,' Dan replied.

Beth stiffened as she heard the slight hesitation in his voice. And he had said *I was*, not *I am*. Was he changing his mind so soon?

Back in Paris, after arranging a quick check-over by a doctor and then debriefing them, Tamara had arranged for a private jet to whisk them back to England so that they could spend Christmas Day with family. Beth had wondered if Dan would say anything to Tamara about quitting the service then, but he hadn't.

In the hot air balloon, floating over the snow-covered French countryside, Dan had promised he was going to give up working for Section 13. Now, only twenty-four hours later, he seemed hesitant, his resolve disappearing.

'You don't sound so sure,' Beth said.

'The thing is, Beth, I've just had an email off Tamara.'

Beth stood back, letting go of Dan. 'An email? Today, of all days? Doesn't that woman ever stop working?'

'Not as far as I know.'

'And what does she say in this email?' Beth asked, her voice taking on an icy tone.

'She says that Section 13 are picking up rumours of another plot by the Order of Omicron.'

'And she wants you to go and investigate.'

'Um, no, actually. She wants you,' Dan said.

'Me?'

'Yes. She thinks you're wonderful; that you were fantastic under pressure, and that you could teach our agents a thing or two. She's sending a car around to pick you up and take you to the airport.'

'No! Seriously?' Beth was having trouble taking all this in. 'But where are we going?'

'Not we. You.' Dan gazed solemnly into Beth's eyes. 'I'm supposed to stay at home to rest and recuperate, while you jet off to Istanbul on a top-secret mission.'

'But I can't go to Istanbul! I've . . . '
Beth turned and looked at the pile of
dirty dishes left on the side. 'I've got to
finish the washing-up,' she said rather
weakly.

Dan broke up into a fit of laughter.

Beth punched him in the arm.
'You're having me on, aren't you?'

'I'm sorry,' Dan gasped. 'But your
face! I wish you could have seen
yourself!'

Beth punched him again, but she was
smiling. 'You really had me going there.
I thought you were serious.'

Dan enveloped his wife in a hug.
'How about we sit down and have a
cup of tea, and a slice of Christmas
cake?'

'That sounds lovely,' Beth replied.
'I'm so glad you're back home. I do
love you, Mr Ogilvy.'

'And I love you, too,' Dan said.

There would be time later to tell
Beth about the email he'd really had
from Tamara. About how she wanted
both Dan and Beth to visit New York in

the New Year, and investigate rumours of a plot to rob the gold bullion centre.

Or maybe he would leave it until tomorrow.

Family came first from now on.

We do hope that you have enjoyed reading this large print book.

Did you know that all of our titles are available for purchase?

We publish a wide range of high quality large print books including:
Romances, Mysteries, Classics
General Fiction
Non Fiction and Westerns

Special interest titles available in large print are:
The Little Oxford Dictionary
Music Book, Song Book
Hymn Book, Service Book

Also available from us courtesy of Oxford University Press:
Young Readers' Dictionary
(large print edition)
Young Readers' Thesaurus
(large print edition)

For further information or a free brochure, please contact us at:
Ulverscroft Large Print Books Ltd.,
The Green, Bradgate Road, Anstey,
Leicester, LE7 7FU, England.
Tel: (00 44) 0116 236 4325
Fax: (00 44) 0116 234 0205

THE RUBY

Fay Cunningham

Cass finds her friend Michael dead in his swimming pool, and while drowning appears at first to be the cause, evidence mounts that foul play was involved. The investigation brings the handsome Detective Inspector Noel Raven into Cass's life — and the connection between the two is literally electrifying. Cass's mother, a witch, warns her that she may be in deadly danger; only by working together can Cass and Noel hope to overcome the evil forces at work. Though Cass finds that her gemstones are also handy in a pinch . . .